Time and the Gods

Lord Dunsany

Table of Contents

Time and the Gods

Lord Dunsany

Kessinger Publishing reprints thousands of hard−to−find books!

TIME AND THE GODS

LORD DUNSANY

1905

PREFACE

These tales are of the things that befell gods and men in Yarnith, Averon, and Zarkandhu, and in the other countries of my dreams.

PART I. TIME AND THE GODS

Once when the gods were young and only Their swarthy servant Time was without age, the gods lay sleeping by a broad river upon earth. There in a valley that from all the earth the gods had set apart for Their repose the gods dreamed marble dreams. And with domes and pinnacles the dreams arose and stood up proudly between the river and the sky, all shimmering white to the morning. In the city's midst the gleaming marble of a thousand steps climbed to the citadel where arose four pinnacles beckoning to heaven, and midmost between the pinnacles there stood the dome, vast, as the gods had dreamed it.

Time and the Gods

All around, terrace by terrace, there went marble lawns well guarded by onyx lions and carved with effigies of all the gods striding amid the symbols of the worlds. With a sound like tinkling bells, far off in a land of shepherds hidden by some hill, the waters of many fountains turned again home. Then the gods awoke and there stood Sardathrion. Not to common men have the gods given to walk Sardathrion's streets, and not to common eyes to see her fountains. Only to those to whom in lonely passes in the night the gods have spoken, leaning through the stars, to those that have heard the voices of the gods above the morning or seen Their faces bending above the sea, only to those hath it been given to see Sardathrion, to stand where her pinnacles gathered together in the night fresh from the dreams of gods. For round the valley a great desert lies through which no common traveller may come, but those whom the gods have chosen feel suddenly a great longing at heart, and crossing the mountains that divide the desert from the world, set out across it driven by the gods, till hidden in the desert's midst they find the valley at last and look with eyes upon Sardathrion.

In the desert beyond the valley grow a myriad thorns, and all pointing towards Sardathrion. So may many that the gods have loved come to the marble city, but none can return, for other cities are no fitting home for men whose feet have touched Sardathrion's marble streets, where even the gods have not been ashamed to come in the guise of men with Their cloaks wrapped about their faces. Therefore no city shall ever hear the songs that are sung in the marble citadel by those in whose ears have rung the voices of the gods. No report shall ever come to other lands of the music of the fall of Sardathrion's fountains, when the waters which went heavenward return again into the lake where the gods cool Their brows sometimes in the guise of men. None may ever hear the speech of the poets of that city, to whom the gods have spoken.

It stands a city aloof. There hath been no rumour of it—I alone have dreamed of it, and I may not be sure that my dreams are true.

* * * * *

Above the Twilight the gods were seated in the after years, ruling the worlds. No longer now They walked at evening in the Marble City hearing the fountains splash, or listening to the singing of the men they loved, because it was in the after years and the work of the gods was to be done.

Time and the Gods

But often as they rested a moment from doing the work of the gods, from hearing the prayers of men or sending here the Pestilence or there Mercy, They would speak awhile with one another of the olden years saying, "Rememberest thou not Sardathrion?" and another would answer "Ah! Sardathrion, and all Sardathrion's mist-draped marble lawns whereon we walk not now."

Then the gods turned to do the work of the gods, answering the prayers of men or smiting them, and ever They sent Their swarthy servant Time to heal or overwhelm. And Time went forth into the worlds to obey the commands of the gods, yet he cast furtive glances at his masters, and the gods distrusted Time because he had known the worlds or ever the gods became.

One day when furtive Time had gone into the worlds to nimbly smite some city whereof the gods were weary, the gods above the twilight speaking to one another said:

"Surely we are the lords of Time and gods of the worlds besides. See how our city Sardathrion lifts over other cities. Others arise and perish but Sardathrion standeth yet, the first and the last of cities. Rivers are lost in the sea and streams forsake the hills, but ever Sardathrion's fountains arise in our dream city. As was Sardathrion when the gods were young, so are her streets to-day as a sign that we are the gods."

Suddenly the swart figure of Time stood up before the gods, with both hands dripping with blood and a red sword dangling idly from his fingers, and said:

"Sardathrion is gone! I have overthrown it!"

And the gods said:

"Sardathrion? Sardathrion, the marble city? Thou, thou hast overthrown it? Thou, the slave of the gods?"

And the oldest of the gods said:

"Sardathrion, Sardathrion, and is Sardathrion gone?"

4

Time and the Gods

And furtively Time looked him in the face and edged towards him fingering with his dripping fingers the hilt of his nimble sword.

Then the gods feared with a new fear that he that had overthrown Their city would one day slay the gods. And a new cry went wailing through the Twilight, the lament of the gods for Their dream city, crying:

"Tears may not bring again Sardathrion.

"But this the gods may do who have seen, and seen with unrelenting eyes, the sorrows of ten thousand worlds—thy gods may weep for thee.

"Tears may not bring again Sardathrion.

"Believe it not, Sardathrion, that ever thy gods sent this doom to thee; he that hath overthrown thee shall overthrow thy gods.

"How oft when Night came suddenly on Morning playing in the fields of Twilight did we watch thy pinnacles emerging from the darkness, Sardathrion, Sardathrion, dream city of the gods, and thine onyx lions looming limb by limb from the dusk.

"How often have we sent our child the Dawn to play with thy fountain tops; how often hath Evening, loveliest of our goddesses, strayed long upon thy balconies.

"Let one fragment of thy marbles stand up above the dust for thine old gods to caress, as a man when all else is lost treasures one lock of the hair of his beloved.

"Sardathrion, the gods must kiss once more the place where thy streets were once.

"There were wonderful marbles in thy streets, Sardathrion."

"Sardathrion, Sardathrion, the gods weep for thee."

THE COMING OF THE SEA

Once there was no sea, and the gods went walking over the green plains of earth.

Upon an evening of the forgotten years the gods were seated on the hills, and all the little rivers of the world lay coiled at Their feet asleep, when Slid, the new god, striding through the stars, came suddenly upon earth lying in a corner of space. And behind Slid there marched a million waves, all following Slid and tramping up the twilight; and Slid touched Earth in one of her great green valleys that divide the south, and here he encamped for the night with all his waves about him. But to the gods as They sat upon Their hilltops a new cry came crying over the green spaces that lay below the hills, and the gods said:

"This is neither the cry of life nor yet the whisper of death. What is this new cry that the gods have never commanded, yet which comes to the ears of the gods?"

And the gods together shouting made the cry of the south, calling the south wind to them. And again the gods shouted all together making the cry of the north, calling the north wind to Them; and thus They gathered to Them all Their winds and sent these four down into the low plains to find what thing it was that called with the new cry, and to drive it away from the gods.

Then all the winds harnessed up their clouds and drave forth till they came to the great green valley that divides the south in twain, and there found Slid with all his waves about him. Then for a space Slid and the four winds struggled with one another till the strength of the winds was gone, and they limped back to the gods, their masters, and said:

"We have met this new thing that has come upon the earth and have striven against its armies, but could not drive them forth; and the new thing is beautiful but very angry, and is creeping towards the gods."

But Slid advanced and led his armies up the valley, and inch by inch and mile by mile he conquered the lands of the gods. Then from Their hills the gods sent down a great array of cliffs against hard, red rocks, and bade them march against Slid. And the cliffs marched down till they came and stood before Slid and leaned their heads forward and

6

frowned and stood staunch to guard the lands of the gods against the might of the sea, shutting Slid off from the world. Then Slid sent some of his smaller waves to search out what stood against him, and the cliffs shattered them. But Slid went back and gathered together a hoard of his greatest waves and hurled them against the cliffs, and the cliffs shattered them. And again Slid called up out of his deep a mighty array of waves and sent them roaring against the guardians of the gods, and the red rocks frowned and smote them. And once again Slid gathered his greater waves and hurled them against the cliffs; and when the waves were scattered like those before them the feet of the cliffs were no longer standing firm, and their faces were scarred and battered. Then into every cleft that stood in the rocks Slid sent his hugest wave and others followed behind it, and Slid himself seized hold of huge rocks with his claws and tore them down and stamped them under his feet. And when the tumult was over the sea had won, and over the broken remnants of those red cliffs the armies of Slid marched on and up the long green valley.

Then the gods heard Slid exulting far away and singing songs of triumph over Their battered cliffs, and ever the tramp of his armies sounded nearer and nearer in the listening ears of the gods.

Then the gods called to Their downlands to save Their world from Slid, and the downlands gathered themselves and marched away, a great white line of gleaming cliffs, and halted before Slid. Then Slid advanced no more and lulled his legions, and while his waves were low he softly crooned a song such as once long ago had troubled the stars and brought down tears out of the twilight.

Sternly the white cliffs stood on guard to save the world of the gods, but the song that once had troubled the stars went moaning on awaking pent desires, till full at the feet of the gods the melody fell. Then the blue rivers that lay curled asleep opened their gleaming eyes, uncurled themselves and shook their rushes, and, making a stir among the hills, crept down to find the sea. And passing across the world they came at last to where the white cliffs stood, and, coming behind them, split them here and there and went through their broken ranks to Slid at last. And the gods were angry with Their traitorous streams.

Then Slid ceased from singing the song that lures the world, and gathered up his legions, and the rivers lifted up their heads with the waves, and all went marching on to assail the cliffs of the gods. And wherever the rivers had broken the ranks of the cliffs, Slid's armies went surging in and broke them up into islands and shattered the islands away. And the gods on Their hill–tops heard once more the voice of Slid exulting over Their cliffs.

Already more than half the world lay subject to Slid, and still his armies advanced; and the people of Slid, the fishes and the long eels, went in and out of arbours that once were dear to the gods. Then the gods feared for Their dominion, and to the innermost sacred recesses of the mountains, to the very heart of the hills, the gods trooped off together and there found Tintaggon, a mountain of black marble, staring far over the earth, and spake thus to him with the voices of the gods:

"O eldest born of our mountains, when first we devised the earth we made thee, and thereafter fashioned fields and hollows, valleys and other hills, to lie about thy feet. And now, Tintaggon, thine ancient lords, the gods, are facing a new thing which overthrows the old. Go therefore, thou, Tintaggon, and stand up against Slid, that the gods be still the gods and the earth still green."

And hearing the voices of his sires, the elder gods, Tintaggon strode down through the evening, leaving a wake of twilight broad behind him as he strode: and going across the green earth came down to Ambrady at the valley's edge, and there met the foremost of Slid's fierce armies conquering the world.

And against him Slid hurled the force of a whole bay, which lashed itself high over Tintaggon's knees and streamed around his flanks and then fell and was lost. Tintaggon still stood firm for the honour and dominion of his lords, the elder gods. Then Slid went to Tintaggon and said: "Let us now make a truce. Stand thou back from Ambrady and let me pass through thy ranks that mine armies may now pass up the valley which opens on the world, that the green earth that dreams around the feet of older gods shall know the new god Slid. Then shall mine armies strive with thee no more, and thou and I shall be the equal lords of the whole earth when all the world is singing the chaunt of Slid, and thy head alone shall be lifted above mine armies when rival hills are dead. And I will deck thee with all the robes of the sea, and all the plunder that I have taken in rare cities shall be piled before thy feet. Tintaggon, I have conquered all the stars, my song swells through all the space besides, I come victorious from Mahn and Khanagat on the furthest edge of the worlds, and thou and I are to be equal lords when the old gods are gone and the green earth knoweth Slid. Behold me gleaming azure and fair with a thousand smiles,

8

and swayed by a thousand moods." And Tintaggon answered: "I am staunch and black and have one mood, and this—to defend my masters and their green earth."

Then Slid went backward growling and summoned together the waves of a whole sea and sent them singing full in Tintaggon's face. Then from Tintaggon's marble front the sea fell backwards crying on to a broken shore, and ripple by ripple straggled back to Slid saying: "Tintaggon stands."

Far out beyond the battered shore that lay at Tintaggon's feet Slid rested long and sent the nautilus to drift up and down before Tintaggon's eyes, and he and his armies sat singing idle songs of dreamy islands far away to the south, and of the still stars whence they had stolen forth, of twilight evenings and of long ago. Still Tintaggon stood with his feet planted fair upon the valley's edge defending the gods and Their green earth against the sea.

And all the while that Slid sang his songs and played with the nautilus that sailed up and down he gathered his oceans together. One morning as Slid sang of old outrageous wars and of most enchanting peace and of dreamy islands and the south wind and the sun, he suddenly launched five oceans out of the deep all to attack Tintaggon. And the five oceans sprang upon Tintaggon and passed above his head. One by one the grip of the oceans loosened, one by one they fell back into the deep and still Tintaggon stood, and on that morning the might of all five oceans lay dead at Tintaggon's feet. That which Slid had conquered he still held, and there is now no longer a great green valley in the south, but all that Tintaggon had guarded against Slid he gave back to the gods. Very calm the sea lies now about Tintaggon's feet, where he stands all black amid crumbled cliffs of white, with red rocks piled about his feet. And often the sea retreats far out along the shore, and often wave by wave comes marching in with the sound of the tramping of armies, that all may still remember the great fight that surged about Tintaggon once, when he guarded the gods and the green earth against Slid.

Sometimes in their dreams the war–scarred warriors of Slid still lift their heads and cry their battle cry; then do dark clouds gather about Tintaggon's swarthy brow and he stands out menacing, seen afar by ships, where once he conquered Slid. And the gods know well that while Tintaggon stands They and Their world are safe; and whether Slid shall one day smite Tintaggon is hidden among the secrets of the sea.

9

A LEGEND OF THE DAWN

When the worlds and All began the gods were stern and old and They saw the Beginning from under eyebrows hoar with years, all but Inzana, Their child, who played with the golden ball. Inzana was the child of all the gods. And the law before the Beginning and thereafter was that all should obey the gods, yet hither and thither went all Pegana's gods to obey the Dawnchild because she loved to be obeyed.

It was dark all over the world and even in Pegana, where dwell the gods, it was dark when the child Inzana, the Dawn, first found her golden ball. Then running down the stairway of the gods with tripping feet, chalcedony, onyx, chalcedony, onyx, step by step, she cast her golden ball across the sky. The golden ball went bounding up the sky, and the Dawnchild with her flaring hair stood laughing upon the stairway of the gods, and it was day. So gleaming fields below saw the first of all the days that the gods have destined. But towards evening certain mountains, afar and aloof, conspired together to stand between the world and the golden ball and to wrap their crags about it and to shut it from the world, and all the world was darkened with their plot. And the Dawnchild up in Pegana cried for her golden ball. Then all the gods came down the stairway right to Pegana's gate to see what ailed the Dawnchild and to ask her why she cried. Then Inzana said that her golden ball had been taken away and hidden by mountains black and ugly, far away from Pegana, all in a world of rocks under the rim of the sky, and she wanted her golden ball and could not love the dark.

Thereat Umborodom, whose hound was the thunder, took his hound in leash, and strode away across the sky after the golden ball until he came to the mountains afar and aloof. There did the thunder put his nose to the rocks and bay along the valleys, and fast at his heels followed Umborodom. And the nearer the hound, the thunder, came to the golden ball the louder did he bay, but haughty and silent stood the mountains whose plot had darkened the world. All in the dark among the crags in a mighty cavern, guarded by two twin peaks, at last they found the golden ball for which the Dawnchild wept. Then under the world went Umborodom with his thunder panting behind him, and came in the dark before the morning from underneath the world and gave the Dawnchild back her golden ball. And Inzana laughed and took it in her hands, and Umborodom went back into Pegana, and at its threshold the thunder went to sleep.

Time and the Gods

Again the Dawnchild tossed the golden ball far up into the blue across the sky, and the second morning shone upon the world, on lakes and oceans, and on drops of dew. But as the ball went bounding on its way, the prowling mists and the rain conspired together and took it and wrapped it in their tattered cloaks and carried it away. And through the rents in their garments gleamed the golden ball, but they held it fast and carried it right away and underneath the world. Then on an onyx step Inzana sat down and wept, who could no more be happy without her golden ball. And again the gods were sorry, and the South Wind came to tell her tales of most enchanted islands, to whom she listened not, nor yet to the tales of temples in lone lands that the East Wind told her, who had stood beside her when she flung her golden ball. But from far away the West Wind came with news of three grey travellers wrapt round with battered cloaks that carried away between them a golden ball.

Then up leapt the North Wind, he who guards the pole, and drew his sword of ice out of his scabbard of snow and sped away along the road that leads across the blue. And in the darkness underneath the world he met the three grey travellers and rushed upon them and drove them far before him, smiting them with his sword till their grey cloaks streamed with blood. And out of the midst of them, as they fled with flapping cloaks all red and grey and tattered, he leapt up with the golden ball and gave it to the Dawnchild.

Again Inzana tossed the ball into the sky, making the third day, and up and up it went and fell towards the fields, and as Inzana stooped to pick it up she suddenly heard the singing of all the birds that were. All the birds in the world were singing all together and also all the streams, and Inzana sat and listened and thought of no golden ball, nor ever of chalcedony and onyx, nor of all her fathers the gods, but only of all the birds. Then in the woods and meadows where they had all suddenly sung, they suddenly ceased. And Inzana, looking up, found that her ball was lost, and all alone in the stillness one owl laughed. When the gods heard Inzana crying for her ball They clustered together on the threshold and peered into the dark, but saw no golden ball. And leaning forward They cried out to the bat as he passed up and down: "Bat that seest all things, where is the golden ball?"

And though the bat answered none heard. And none of the winds had seen it nor any of the birds, and there were only the eyes of the gods in the darkness peering for the golden ball. Then said the gods: "Thou hast lost thy golden ball," and They made her a moon of silver to roll about the sky. And the child cried and threw it upon the stairway and chipped and broke its edges and asked for the golden ball. And Limpang Tung, the Lord of Music, who was least of all the gods, because the child cried still for her golden ball, stole out of Pegana and crept across the sky, and found the birds of all the world sitting in trees and ivy, and whispering in the dark. He asked them one by one for news of the golden ball. Some had last seen it on a neighbouring hill and others in trees, though none knew where it was. A heron had seen it lying in a pond, but a wild duck in some reeds had seen it last as she came home across the hills, and then it was rolling very far away.

At last the cock cried out that he had seen it lying beneath the world. There Limpang Tung sought it and the cock called to him through the darkness as he went, until at last he found the golden ball. Then Limpang Tung went up into Pegana and gave it to the Dawnchild, who played with the moon no more. And the cock and all his tribe cried out: "We found it. We found the golden ball."

Again Inzana tossed the ball afar, laughing with joy to see it, her hands stretched upwards, her golden hair afloat, and carefully she watched it as it fell. But alas! it fell with a splash into the great sea and gleamed and shimmered as it fell till the waters became dark above it and could be seen no more. And men on the world said: "How the dew has fallen, and how the mists set in with breezes from the streams."

But the dew was the tears of the Dawnchild, and the mists were her sighs when she said: "There will no more come a time when I play with my ball again, for now it is lost for ever."

And the gods tried to comfort Inzana as she played with her silver moon, but she would not hear Them, and went in tears to Slid, where he played with gleaming sails, and in his mighty treasury turned over gems and pearls and lorded it over the sea. And she said: "O Slid, whose soul is in the sea, bring back my golden ball."

And Slid stood up, swarthy, and clad in seaweed, and mightily dived from the last chalcedony step out of Pegana's threshold straight into ocean. There on the sand, among the battered navies of the nautilus and broken weapons of the swordfish, hidden by dark water, he found the golden ball. And coming up in the night, all green and dripping, he carried it gleaming to the stairway of the gods and brought it back to Inzana from the sea; and out of the hands of Slid she took it and tossed it far and wide over his sails and sea, and far away it shone on lands that knew not Slid, till it came to its zenith and dropped towards the world.

But ere it fell the Eclipse dashed out from his hiding, and rushed at the golden ball and seized it in his jaws. When Inzana saw the Eclipse bearing her plaything away she cried aloud to the thunder, who burst from Pegana and fell howling upon the throat of the Eclipse, who dropped the golden ball and let it fall towards earth. But the black mountains disguised themselves with snow, and as the golden ball fell down towards them they turned their peaks to ruby crimson and their lakes to sapphires gleaming amongst silver, and Inzana saw a jewelled casket into which her plaything fell. But when she stooped to pick it up again she found no jewelled casket with rubies, silver or sapphires, but only wicked mountains disguised in snow that had trapped her golden ball. And then she cried because there was none to find it, for the thunder was far away chasing the Eclipse, and all the gods lamented when They saw her sorrow. And Limpang Tung, who was least of all the gods, was yet the saddest at the Dawnchild's grief, and when the gods said: "Play with your silver moon," he stepped lightly from the rest, and coming down the stairway of the gods, playing an instrument of music, went out towards the world to find the golden ball because Inzana wept.

And into the world he went till he came to the nether cliffs that stand by the inner mountains in the soul and heart of the earth where the Earthquake dwelleth alone, asleep but astir as he sleeps, breathing and moving his legs, and grunting aloud in the dark. Then in the ear of the Earthquake Limpang Tung said a word that only the gods may say, and the Earthquake started to his feet and flung the cave away, the cave wherein he slept between the cliffs, and shook himself and went galloping abroad and overturned the mountains that hid the golden ball, and bit the earth beneath them and hurled their crags about and covered himself with rocks and fallen hills, and went back ravening and growling into the soul of the earth, and there lay down and slept again for a hundred years. And the golden ball rolled free, passing under the shattered earth, and so rolled back to Pegana; and Limpang Tung came home to the onyx step and took the Dawnchild by the hand and told not what he had done but said it was the Earthquake, and went away to sit at the feet of the gods. But Inzana went and patted the Earthquake on the head, for she said it was dark and lonely in the soul of the earth. Thereafter, returning step by step, chalcedony, onyx, chalcedony, onyx, up the stairway of the gods, she cast again her golden ball from the Threshold afar into the blue to gladden the world and the sky, and laughed to see it go.

Time and the Gods

And far away Trogool upon the utter Rim turned a page that was numbered six in a cipher that none might read. And as the golden ball went through the sky to gleam on lands and cities, there came the Fog towards it, stooping as he walked with his dark brown cloak about him, and behind him slunk the Night. And as the golden ball rolled past the Fog suddenly Night snarled and sprang upon it and carried it away. Hastily Inzana gathered the gods and said: "The Night hath seized my golden ball and no god alone can find it now, for none can say how far the Night may roam, who prowls all round us and out beyond the worlds."

At the entreaty of Their Dawnchild all the gods made Themselves stars for torches, and far away through all the sky followed the tracks of Night as far as he prowled abroad. And at one time Slid, with the Pleiades in his hand, came nigh to the golden ball, and at another Yoharneth–Lahai, holding Orion for a torch, but lastly Limpang Tung, bearing the morning star, found the golden ball far away under the world near to the lair of Night.

And all the gods together seized the ball, and Night turning smote out the torches of the gods and thereafter slunk away; and all the gods in triumph marched up the gleaming stairway of the gods, all praising little Limpang Tung, who through the chase had followed Night so close in search of the golden ball. Then far below on the world a human child cried out to the Dawnchild for the golden ball, and Inzana ceased from her play that illumined world and sky, and cast the ball from the Threshold of the gods to the little human child that played in the fields below, and would one day die. And the child played all day long with the golden ball down in the little fields where the humans lived, and went to bed at evening and put it beneath his pillow, and went to sleep, and no one worked in all the world because the child was playing. And the light of the golden ball streamed up from under the pillow and out through the half shut door and shone in the western sky, and Yoharneth–Lahai in the night time tip–toed into the room, and took the ball gently (for he was a god) away from under the pillow and brought it back to the Dawnchild to gleam on an onyx step.

But some day Night shall seize the golden ball and carry it right away and drag it down to his lair, and Slid shall dive from the Threshold into the sea to see if it be there, and coming up when the fishermen draw their nets shall find it not, nor yet discover it among the sails. Limpang Tung shall seek among the birds and shall not find it when the cock is mute, and up the valleys shall go Umborodom to seek among the crags. And the hound, the thunder, shall chase the Eclipse and all the gods go seeking with Their stars, but never find the ball. And men, no longer having light of the golden ball, shall pray to the gods no more, who, having no worship, shall be no more the gods.

These things be hidden even from the gods.

THE VENGEANCE OF MEN

Ere the Beginning the gods divided earth into waste and pasture. Pleasant pastures They made to be green over the face of earth, orchards They made in valleys and heather upon hills, but Harza They doomed, predestined and foreordained to be a waste for ever.

When the world prayed at evening to the gods and the gods answered prayers They forgot the prayers of all the Tribes of Arim. Therefore the men of Arim were assailed with wars and driven from land to land and yet would not be crushed. And the men of Arim made them gods for themselves, appointing men as gods until the gods of Pegana should remember them again. And their leaders, Yoth and Haneth, played the part of gods and led their people on though every tribe assailed them. At last they came to Harza, where no tribes were, and at last had rest from war, and Yoth and Haneth said: "The work is done, and surely now Pegana's gods will remember." And they built a city in Harza and tilled the soil, and the green came over the waste as the wind comes over the sea, and there were fruit and cattle in Harza and the sounds of a million sheep. There they rested from their flight from all the tribes, and builded fables out of all their sorrows till all men smiled in Harza and children laughed.

Then said the gods, "Earth is no place for laughter." Thereat They strode to Pegana's outer gate, to where the Pestilence lay curled asleep, and waking him up They pointed toward Harza, and the Pestilence leapt forward howling across the sky.

That night he came to the fields near Harza, and stalking through the grass sat down and glared at the lights, and licked his paws and glared at the lights again.

But the next night, unseen, through laughing crowds, the Pestilence crept into the city, and stealing into the houses one by one, peered into the people's eyes, looking even through their eyelids, so that when morning came men stared before them crying out that they saw the Pestilence whom others saw not, and thereafter died, because the green eyes of the Pestilence had looked into their souls. Chill and damp was he, yet there came heat from his eyes that parched the souls of men. Then came the physicians and the men learned in magic, and made the sign of the physicians and the sign of the men of magic and cast blue water upon herbs and chanted spells; but still the Pestilence crept from house to house and still he looked into the souls of men. And the lives of the people streamed away from Harza, and whither they went is set in many books. But the Pestilence fed on the light that shines in the eyes of men, which never appeased his hunger; chiller and damper he grew, and the heat from his eyes increased when night by night he galloped through the city, going by stealth no more.

Then did men pray in Harza to the gods, saying:

"High gods! Show clemency to Harza."

And the gods listened to their prayers, but as They listened They pointed with their fingers and cheered the Pestilence on. And the Pestilence grew bolder at his masters' voices and thrust his face close up before the eyes of men.

He could be seen by none saving those he smote. At first he slept by day, lying in misty hollows, but as his hunger increased he sprang up even in sunlight and clung to the chests of men and looked down through their eyes into their souls that shrivelled, until almost he could be dimly seen even by those he smote not.

Adro, the physician, sat in his chamber with one light burning, making a mixing in a bowl that should drive the Pestilence away, when through his door there blew a draught that set the light a–flickering.

Then because the draught was cold the physician shivered and went and closed the door, but as he turned again he saw the Pestilence lapping at his mixing, who sprang and set one paw upon Adro's shoulder and another upon his cloak, while with two he clung to his waist, and looked him in the eyes.

Two men were walking in the street; one said to the other: "Upon the morrow I will sup with thee."

Time and the Gods

And the Pestilence grinned a grin that none beheld, baring his dripping teeth, and crept away to see whether upon the morrow those men should sup together.

A traveller coming in said: "This is Harza. Here will I rest."

But his life went further than Harza upon that day's journey.

All feared the Pestilence, and those that he smote beheld him, but none saw the great shapes of the gods by starlight as They urged Their Pestilence on.

Then all men fled from Harza, and the Pestilence chased dogs and rats and sprang upward at the bats as they sailed above him, who died and lay in the streets. But soon he returned and pursued the men of Harza where they fled, and sat by rivers where they came to drink, away below the city. Then back to Harza went the people of Harza pursued by the Pestilence still, and gathered in the Temple of All the gods save One, and said to the High Prophet: "What may now be done?" who answered:

"All the gods have mocked at prayer. This sin must now be punished by the vengeance of men."

And the people stood in awe.

The High Prophet went up to the Tower beneath the sky whereupon beat the eyes of all the gods by starlight. There in the sight of the gods he spake in the ear of the gods, saying: "High gods! Ye have made mock of men. Know therefore that it is writ in ancient lore and found by prophecy that there is an *End* that waiteth for the gods, who shall go down from Pegana in galleons of gold all down the Silent River and into the Silent Sea, and there Their galleons shall go up in mist and They shall be gods no more. And men shall gain harbour from the mocking of the gods at last in the warm moist earth, but to the gods shall no ceasing ever come from being the Things that were the gods. When Time and worlds and death are gone away nought shall then remain but worn regrets and Things that were once gods.

"In the sight of the gods.

"In the ear of the gods."

Then the gods shouted all together and pointed with Their hands at the High Prophet's throat, and the Pestilence sprang.

Long since the High Prophet is dead and his words are forgotten by men, but the gods know not yet whether it be true that *The End* is waiting for the gods, and him who might have told Them They have slain. And the gods of Pegana are fearing the fear that hath fallen upon the gods because of the vengeance of men, for They know not when *The End* shall be, or whether it shall come.

WHEN THE GODS SLEPT

All the gods were sitting in Pegana, and Their slave, Time, lay idle at Pegana's gate with nothing to destroy, when They thought of worlds, worlds large and round and gleaming, and little silver moons. Then (who knoweth when?), as the gods raised Their hands making the sign of the gods, the thoughts of the gods became worlds and silver moons. And the worlds swam by Pegana's gate to take their places in the sky, to ride at anchor for ever, each where the gods had bidden. And because they were round and big and gleamed all over the sky, the gods laughed and shouted and all clapped Their hands. Then upon earth the gods played out the game of the gods, the game of life and death, and on the other worlds They did a secret thing, playing a game that is hidden.

At last They mocked no more at life and laughed at death no more, and cried aloud in Pegana: "Will no new thing be? Must those four march for ever round the world till our eyes are wearied with the treading of the feet of the Seasons that will not cease, while Night and Day and Life and Death drearily rise and fall?"

And as a child stares at the bare walls of a narrow hut, so the gods looked all listlessly upon the worlds, saying:

"Will no new thing be?"

And in Their weariness the gods said: "Ah! to be young again. Ah! to be fresh once more from the brain of *Mana—Yood—Sushai*."

And They turned away Their eyes in weariness from all the gleaming worlds and laid

18

Time and the Gods

Them down upon Pegana's floor, for They said:

"It may be that the worlds shall pass and we would fain forget them."

Then the gods slept. Then did the comet break loose from his moorings and the eclipse roamed about the sky, and down on the earth did Death's three children—Famine, Pestilence, and Drought—come out to feed. The eyes of the Famine were green, and the eyes of the Drought were red, but the Pestilence was blind and smote about all round him with his claws among the cities.

But as the gods slept, there came from beyond the Rim, out of the dark and unknown, three Yozis, spirits of ill, that sailed up the river of Silence in galleons with silver sails. Far away they had seen Yum and Gothum, the stars that stand sentinel over Pegana's gate, blinking and falling asleep, and as they neared Pegana they found a hush wherein the gods slept heavily. Ya, Ha, and Snyrg were these three Yozis, the lords of evil, madness, and of spite. When they crept from their galleons and stole over Pegana's silent threshold it boded ill for the gods. There in Pegana lay the gods asleep, and in a corner lay the Power of the gods alone upon the floor, a thing wrought of black rock and four words graven upon it, whereof I might not give thee any clue, if even I should find it—four words of which none knoweth. Some say they tell of the opening of a flower towards dawn, and others say they concern earthquakes among hills, and others that they tell of the death of fishes, and others that the words be these: Power, Knowledge, Forgetting, and another word that not the gods themselves may ever guess. These words the Yozis read, and sped away in dread lest the gods should wake, and going aboard their galleons, bade the rowers haste. Thus the Yozis became gods, having the power of gods, and they sailed away to the earth, and came to a mountainous island in the sea. There they sat upon the rocks, sitting as the gods sit, with their right hands uplifted, and having the power of gods, only none came to worship. Thither came no ships nigh them, nor ever at evening came the prayers of men, nor smell of incense, nor screams from the sacrifice. Then said the Yozis:

"Of what avails it that we be gods if no one worship us nor give us sacrifice?"

And Ya, Ha, and Snyrg set sail in their silver galleons, and went looming down the sea to come to the shores of men. And first they came to an island where were fisher folk; and the folk of the island, running down to the shore cried out to them:

Time and the Gods

"Who be ye?"

And the Yozis answered:

"We be three gods, and we would have your worship."

But the fisher folk answered:

"Here we worship Rahm, the Thunder, and have no worship nor sacrifice for other gods."

Then the Yozis snarled with anger and sailed away, and sailed till they came to another shore, sandy and low and forsaken. And at last they found an old man upon the shore, and they cried out to him:

"Old man upon the shore! We be three gods that it were well to worship, gods of great power and apt in the granting of prayer."

The old man answered:

"We worship Pegana's gods, who have a fondness for our incense and the sound of our sacrifice when it squeals upon the altar."

Then answered Snyrg:

"Asleep are Pegana's gods, nor will They wake for the humming of thy prayers which lie in the dust upon Pegana's floor, and over Them Sniracte, the spider of the worlds, hath woven a web of mist. And the squealing of the sacrifice maketh no music in ears that are closed in sleep."

The old man answered, standing upon the shore:

"Though all the gods of old shall answer our prayers no longer, yet still to the gods of old shall all men pray here in Syrinais."

But the Yozis turned their ships about and angrily sailed away, all cursing Syrinais and Syrinais's gods, but most especially the old man that stood upon the shore.

20

Time and the Gods

Still the three Yozis lusted for the worship of men, and came, on the third night of their sailing, to a city's lights; and nearing the shore they found it a city of song wherein all folks rejoiced. Then sat each Yozi on his galleon's prow, and leered with his eyes upon the city, so that the music stopped and the dancing ceased, and all looked out to sea at the strange shapes of the Yozis beneath their silver sails. Then Snyrg demanded their worship, promising increase of joys, and swearing by the light of his eyes that he would send little flames to leap over the grass, to pursue the enemies of that city and to chase them about the world.

But the people answered that in that city men worshipped Agrodaun, the mountain standing alone, and might not worship other gods even though they came in galleons with silver sails, sailing from over the sea. But Snyrg answered:

"Certainly Agrodaun is only a mountain, and in no manner a god."

But the priests of Agrodaun sang answer from the shore:

"If the sacrifice of men make not Agrodaun a god, nor blood still young on his rocks, nor the little fluttering prayers of ten thousand hearts, nor two thousands years of worship and all the hopes of the people and the whole strength of our race, then are there no gods and ye be common sailors, sailing from over the sea."

Then said the Yozis:

"Hath Agrodaun answered prayer?" And the people heard the words that the Yozis said.

Then went the priests of Agrodaun away from the shore and up the steep streets of the city, the people following, and over the moor beyond it to the foot of Agrodaun, and then said:

"Agrodaun, if thou art not our god, go back and herd with yonder common hills, and put a cap of snow upon thy head and crouch far off as they do beneath the sky; but if we have given thee divinity in two thousand years, if our hopes are all about thee like a cloak, then stand and look upon thy worshippers from over our city for ever." And the smoke that ascended from his feet stood still and there fell a hush over great Agrodaun; and the priests went back to the sea and said to the three Yozis:

Time and the Gods

"New gods shall have our worship when Agrodaun grows weary of being our god, or when in some night–time he shall stride away, leaving us nought to gaze at that is higher than our city."

And the Yozis sailed away and cursed towards Agrodaun, but could not hurt him, for he was but a mountain.

And the Yozis sailed along the coast till they came to a river running to the sea, and they sailed up the river till they came to a people at work, who furrowed the soil and sowed, and strove against the forest. Then the Yozis called to the people as they worked in the fields:

"Give us your worship and ye shall have many joys."

But the people answered:

"We may not worship you."

Then answered Snyrg:

"Ye also, have ye a god?"

And the people answered:

"We worship the years to come, and we set the world in order for their coming, as one layeth raiment on the road before the advent of a King. And when those years shall come, they shall accept the worship of a race they knew not, and their people shall make their sacrifice to the years that follow them, who, in their turn, shall minister to the *End*."

Then answered Snyrg:

"Gods that shall recompense you not. Rather give us your prayers and have our pleasures, the pleasures that we shall give you, and when your gods shall come, let them be wroth—they cannot punish you."

Time and the Gods

But the people continued to sacrifice their labour to their gods, the years to come, making the world a place for gods to dwell in, and the Yozis cursed those gods and sailed away. And Ya, the Lord of malice, swore that when those years should come, they should see whether it were well for them to have snatched away the worship from three Yozis.

And still the Yozis sailed, for they said:

"It were better to be birds and have no air to fly in, than to be gods having neither prayers nor worship."

But where sky met with ocean, the Yozis saw land again, and thither sailed; and there the Yozis saw men in strange old garments performing ancient rites in a land of many temples. And the Yozis called to the men as they performed their ancient rites and said:

"We be three gods well versed in the needs of men, to worship whom were to obtain instant joy."

But the men said:

"We have already gods."

And Snyrg replied:

"Ye, too?"

The men answered:

"For we worship the things that have been and all the years that were. Divinely have they helped us, therefore we give them worship that is their due."

And the Yozis answered the people:

"We be gods of the present and return good things for worship."

But the people answered, saying from the shore:

Time and the Gods

"Our gods have given us already the good things, and we return Them the worship that is Their due."

And the Yozis set their faces to landward, and cursed all things that had been and all the years that were, and sailed in their galleons away.

A rocky shore in an inhuman land stood up against the sea. Thither the Yozis came and found no man, but out of the dark from inland towards evening came a herd of great baboons and chattered greatly when they saw the ships.

Then spake Snyrg to them:

"Have ye, too, a god?"

And the baboons spat.

Then said the Yozis:

"We be seductive gods, having a particular remembrance for little prayers."

But the baboons leered fiercely at the Yozis and would have none of them for gods.

One said that prayers hindered the eating of nuts. But Snyrg leaned forward and whispered, and the baboons went down upon their knees and clasped their hands as men clasp, and chattered prayer and said to one another that these were the gods of old, and gave the Yozis their worship—for Snyrg had whispered in their ears that, if they would worship the Yozis, he would make them men. And the baboons arose from worshipping, smoother about the face and a little shorter in the arms, and went away and hid their bodies in clothing, and afterwards galloped away from the rocky shore and went and herded with men. And men could not discern what they were, for their bodies were bodies of men, though their souls were still the souls of beasts and their worship went to the Yozis, spirits of ill.

And the lords of malice, hatred and madness sailed back to their island in the sea and sat upon the shore as gods sit, with right hand uplifted; and at evening foul prayers from the baboons gathered about them and infested the rocks.

But in Pegana the gods awoke with a start.

THE KING THAT WAS NOT

The land of Runazar hath no King nor ever had one; and this is the law of the land of Runazar that, seeing that it hath never had a King, it shall not have one for ever. Therefore in Runazar the priests hold sway, who tell people that never in Runazar hath there been a King.

Althazar, King of Runazar, and lord of all lands near by, commanded for the closer knowledge of the gods that Their images should be carven in Runazar, and in all lands near by. And when Althazar's command, wafted abroad by trumpets, came tinkling in the ear of all the gods, right glad were They at the sound of it. Therefore men quarried marble from the earth, and sculptors busied themselves in Runazar to obey the edict of the King. But the gods stood by starlight on the hills where the sculptors might see Them, and draped the clouds about Them, and put upon Them Their divinest air, that sculptors might do justice to Pegana's gods. Then the gods strode back into Pegana and the sculptors hammered and wrought, and there came a day when the Master of Sculptors took audience of the King, saying:

"Althazar, King of Runazar, High Lord moreover of all the lands near by, to whom be the gods benignant, humbly have we completed the images of all such gods as were in thine edict named."

Then the King commanded a great space to be cleared among the houses in his city, and there the images of all the gods were borne and set before the King, and there were assembled the Master of Sculptors and all his men; and before each stood a soldier bearing a pile of gold upon a jewelled tray, and behind each stood a soldier with a drawn sword pointing against their necks, and the King looked upon the images. And lo! they stood as gods with the clouds all draped about them, making the sign of the gods, but their bodies were those of men, and lo! their faces were very like the King's, and their beards were as the King's beard. And the King said:

"These be indeed Pegana's gods."

And the soldiers that stood before the sculptors were caused to present to them the piles of gold, and the soldiers that stood behind the sculptors were caused to sheath their swords. And the people shouted:

"These be indeed Pegana's gods, whose faces we are permitted to see by the will of Althazar the King, to whom be the gods benignant." And heralds were sent abroad through the cities of Runazar and of all the lands near by, proclaiming of the images:

"These be Pegana's gods."

But up in Pegana the gods howled with wrath and Mung leant forward to make the sign of Mung against Althazar the King. But the gods laid Their hands upon his shoulder saying:

"Slay him not, for it is not enough that Althazar shall die, who hath made the faces of the gods to be like the faces of men, but he must not even have ever been."

Then said the gods:

"Spake we of Althazar, a King?"

And the gods said:

"Nay, we spake not." And the gods said:

"Dreamed we of one Althazar?" And the gods said:

"Nay, we dreamed not."

But in the royal palace of Runazar, Althazar, passing suddenly out of the remembrance of the gods, became no longer a thing that was or had ever been.

And by the throne of Althazar lay a robe, and near it lay a crown, and the priests of the gods entered his palace and made it a temple of the gods. And the people coming to worship said:

"Whose was this robe and to what purpose is this crown?"

And the priests answered:

"The gods have cast away the fragment of a garment and lo! from the fingers of the gods hath slipped one little ring."

And the people said to the priests:

"Seeing that Runazar hath never had a King, therefore be ye our rulers, and make ye our laws in the sight of Pegana's gods."

THE CAVE OF KAI

The pomp of crowning was ended, the rejoicings had died away, and Khanazar, the new King, sat in the seat of the Kings of Averon to do his work upon the destinies of men. His uncle, Khanazar the Lone, had died, and he had come from a far castle to the south, with a great procession, to Ilaun, the citadel of Averon; and there they had crowned him King of Averon and of the mountains, and Lord, if there be aught beyond those mountains, of all such lands as are. But now the pomp of the crowning was gone away and Khanazar sat afar off from his home, a very mighty King.

Then the King grew weary of the destinies of Averon and weary of the making of commands. So Khanazar sent heralds through all cities saying:

"Hear! The will of the King! Hear! The will of the King of Averon and of the mountains and Lord, if there be aught beyond those mountains, of all such lands as are. Let there come together to Ilaun all such as have an art in secret matters. Hear!"

And there gathered together to Ilaun the wise men of all the degrees of magic, even to the seventh, who had made spells before Khanazar the Lone; and they came before the new King in his palace placing their hands upon his feet. Then said the King to the magicians:

"I have a need."

27

Time and the Gods

And they answered:

"The earth touches the feet of the King in token of submission."

But the King answered:

"My need is not of the earth; but I would find certain of the hours that have been, and sundry days that were."

And all the wise folks were silent, till there spake out mournfully the wisest of them all, who made spells in the seventh degree, saying:

"The days that were, and the hours, have winged their way to Mount Agdora's summit, and there, dipping, have passed away from sight, not ever to return, for haply they have not heard the King's command."

Of these wise folks are many things chronicled. Moreover, it is set in writing of the scribes how they had audience of King Khanazar and of the words they spake, but of their further deeds there is no legend. But it is told how the King sent men to run and pass through all the cities till they should find one that was wiser even than the magicians that had made spells before Khanazar the Lone. Far up the mountains that limit Averon they found Syrahn, the prophet, among the goats, who was of none of the degrees of magic, and who had cast no spells before the former King. Him they brought to Khanazar, and the King said unto him:

"I have a need."

And Syrahn answered:

"Thou art a man."

And the King said:

"Where lie the days that were and certain hours?"

And Syrahn answered:

28

Time and the Gods

"These things lie in a cave afar from here, and over the cave stands sentinel one Kai, and this cave Kai hath guarded from the gods and men since ever the Beginning was made. It may be that he shall let Khanazar pass by."

Then the King gathered elephants and camels that carried burdens of gold, and trusty servants that carried precious gems, and gathered an army to go before him and an army to follow behind, and sent out horsemen to warn the dwellers of the plains that the King of Averon was afoot.

And he bade Syrahn to lead to that place where the days of old lie hid and all forgotten hours.

Across the plain and up Mount Agdora, and dipping beyond its summit went Khanazar the King, and his two armies who followed Syrahn. Eight times the purple tent with golden border had been pitched for the King of Averon, and eight times it had been struck ere the King and the King's armies came to a dark cave in a valley dark, where Kai stood guard over the days that were. And the face of Kai was as a warrior that vanquisheth cities and burdeneth himself not with captives, and his form was as the forms of gods, but his eyes were the eyes of beasts; before whom came the King of Averon with elephants and camels bearing burdens of gold, and trusty servants carrying precious gems.

Then said the King:

"Yonder behold my gifts. Give back to me my yesterday with its waving banners, my yesterday with its music and blue sky and all its cheering crowds that made me King, the yesterday that sailed with gleaming wings over my Averon."

And Kai answered, pointing to his cave:

"Thither, dishonoured and forgot, thy yesterday slunk away. And who amid the dusty heap of the forgotten days shall grovel to find thy yesterday?"

Then answered the King of Averon and of the mountains and Lord, if there be aught beyond them, of all such lands as are:

29

Time and the Gods

"I will go down on my knees in yon dark cave and search with my hands amid the dust, if so I may find my yesterday again and certain hours that are gone."

And the King pointed to his piles of gold that stood where elephants were met together, and beyond them to the scornful camels. And Kai answered:

"The gods have offered me the gleaming worlds and all as far as the Rim, and whatever lies beyond it as far as the gods may see—and thou comest to me with elephants and camels."

Then said the King:

"Across the orchards of my home there hath passed one hour whereof thou knowest well, and I pray to thee, who wilt take no gifts borne upon elephants or camels, to give me of thy mercy one second back, one grain of dust that clings to that hour in the heap that lies within thy cave."

And, at the word mercy, Kai laughed. And the King turned his armies to the east. Therefore the armies returned to Averon and the heralds before them cried:

"Here cometh Khanazar, King of Averon and of the mountains and Lord, if there be aught beyond those mountains, of all such lands as are."

And the King said to them:

"Say rather that here comes one greatly wearied who, having accomplished nought, returneth from a quest forlorn."

So the King came again to Averon.

But it is told how there came into Ilaun one evening as the sun was setting a harper with a golden harp desiring audience of the King.

And it is told how men led him to Khanazar, who sat frowning alone upon his throne, to whom said the harper:

Time and the Gods

"I have a golden harp; and to its strings have clung like dust some seconds out of the forgotten hours and little happenings of the days that were."

And Khanazar looked up and the harper touched the strings, and the old forgotten things were stirring again, and there arose a sound of songs that had passed away and long since voices. Then when the harper saw that Khanazar looked not angrily upon him his fingers tramped over the chords as the gods tramp down the sky, and out of the golden harp arose a haze of memories; and the King leaning forward and staring before him saw in the haze no more his palace walls, but saw a valley with a stream that wandered through it, and woods upon either hill, and an old castle standing lonely to the south. And the harper, seeing a strange look upon the face of Khanazar, said:

"Is the King pleased who lords it over Averon and the mountains, and, if there be aught beyond them, over all such lands as are?"

And the King said:—

"Seeing that I am a child again in a valley to the south, how may I say what may be the will of the great King?"

When the stars shone high over Ilaun and still the King sat staring straight before him, all the courtiers drew away from the great palace, save one that stayed and kept one taper burning, and with them went the harper.

And when the dawn came up through silent archways into the marble palace, making the taper pale, the King still stared before him, and still he sat there when the stars shone again clearly and high above Ilaun.

But on the second morning the King arose and sent for the harper and said to him:—

"I am King again, and thou that hast a skill to stay the hours and mayest may bring again to men their forgotten days, thou shalt stand sentinel over my great to-morrow; and when I go forth to conquer Ziman-ho and make my armies mighty thou shalt stand between that morrow and the cave of Kai, and haply some deed of mine and the battling of my armies shall cling to thy golden harp and not go down dishonoured into the cave. For my to-morrow, who with such resounding stride goes trampling through my dreams, is far too kingly to herd with forgotten days in the dust of things that were. But on some future day, when Kings are dead and all their deeds forgotten, some harper of that time shall come and from those golden strings awake those deeds that echo in my dreams, till my to–morrow shall stride forth among the lesser days and tell the years that Khanazar was a King."

And answered the harper:

"I will stand sentinel over thy great to–morrow, and when thou goest forth to conquer Ziman–ho and make thine armies mighty I will stand between thy morrow and the cave of Kai, till thy deeds and the battling of thine armies shall cling to my golden harp and not go down dishonoured into the cave. So that when Kings are dead and all their deeds forgotten the harpers of the future time shall awake from these golden chords those deeds of thine. This will I do."

Men of these days, that be skilled upon the harp, tell still of Khanazar, how that he was King of Averon and of the mountains, and claimed lordship of certain lands beyond, and how he went with armies against Ziman–ho and fought great battles, and in the last gained victory and was slain. But Kai, as he waited with his claws to gather in the last days of Khanazar that they might loom enormous in his cave, still found them not, and only gathered in some meaner deeds and the days and hours of lesser men, and was vexed by the shadow of a harper that stood between him and the world.

THE SORROW OF SEARCH

It is told also of King Khanazar how he bowed very low unto the gods of Old. None bowed so low unto the gods of Old as did King Khanazar.

One day the King returning from the worship of the gods of Old and from bowing before them in the temple of the gods commanded their prophets to appear before him, saying:

"I would know somewhat concerning the gods."

Then came the prophets before King Khanazar, burdened with many books, to whom the King said:

Time and the Gods

"It is not in books."

Thereat the prophets departed, bearing away with them a thousand methods well devised in books whereby men may gain wisdom of the gods. One alone remained, a master prophet, who had forgotten books, to whom the King said:

"The gods of Old are mighty."

And answered the master prophet:

"Very mighty are the gods of Old."

Then said the King:

"There are no gods but the gods of Old."

And answered the prophet:

"There are none other."

And they two being alone within the palace the King said:

"Tell me aught concerning gods or men if aught of the truth be known."

Then said the master prophet:

"Far and white and straight lieth the road to Knowing, and down it in the heat and dust go all wise people of the earth, but in the fields before they come to it the very wise lie down or pluck the flowers. By the side of the road to Knowing—O King, it is hard and hot—stand many temples, and in the doorway of every temple stand many priests, and they cry to the travellers that weary of the road, crying to them:

"This is the End."

And in the temples are the sounds of music, and from each roof arises the savour of pleasant burning; and all that look at a cool temple, whichever temple they look at, or

Time and the Gods

hear the hidden music, turn in to see whether it be indeed the End. And such as find that their temple is not indeed the End set forth again upon the dusty road, stopping at each temple as they pass for fear they miss the End, or striving onwards on the road, and see nothing in the dust, till they can walk no longer and are taken worn and weary of their journey into some other temple by a kindly priest who shall tell them that this also is the End. Neither on that road may a man gain any guiding from his fellows, for only one thing that they say is surely true, when they say:

"Friend, we can see nothing for the dust."

And of the dust that hides the way much has been there since ever that road began, and some is stirred up by the feet of all that travel upon it, and more arises from the temple doors.

And, O King, it were better for thee, travelling upon that road, to rest when thou hearest one calling: "This is the End," with the sounds of music behind him. And if in the dust and darkness thou pass by Lo and Mush and the pleasant temple of Kynash, or Sheenath with his opal smile, or Sho with his eyes of agate, yet Shilo and Mynarthitep, Gazo and Amurund and Slig are still before thee and the priests of their temples will not forget to call thee.

And, O King, it is told that only one discerned the end and passed by three thousand temples, and the priests of the last were like the priests of the first, and all said that their temple was at the end of the road, and the dark of the dust lay over them all, and all were very pleasant and only the road was weary. And in some were many gods, and in a few only one, and in some the shrine was empty, and all had many priests, and in all the travellers were happy as they rested. And into some his fellow travellers tried to force him, and when he said:

"I will travel further," many said:

"This man lies, for the road ends here."

And he that travelled to the End hath told that when the thunder was heard upon the road there arose the sound of the voices of all the priests as far as he could hear, crying:

Time and the Gods

"Hearken to Shilo"—"Hear Mush"—"Lo! Kynash"—"The voice of Sho"—"Mynarthitep is angry"—"Hear the word of Slig!"

And far away along the road one cried to the traveller that Sheenath stirred in his sleep.

O King this is very doleful. It is told that that traveller came at last to the utter End and there was a mighty gulf, and in the darkness at the bottom of the gulf one small god crept, no bigger than a hare, whose voice came crying in the cold:

"I know not."

And beyond the gulf was nought, only the small god crying.

And he that travelled to the End fled backwards for a great distance till he came to temples again, and entering one where a priest cried:

"This is the End," lay down and rested on a couch. There Yush sat silent, carved with an emerald tongue and two great eyes of sapphire, and there many rested and were happy. And an old priest, coming from comforting a child, came over to that traveller who had seen the End and said to him:

"This is Yush and this is the End of wisdom."

And the traveller answered:

"Yush is very peaceful and this indeed the End."

"O King, wouldst thou hear more?"

And the King said:

"I would hear all."

And the master prophet answered:

Time and the Gods

"There was also another prophet and his name was Shaun, who had such reverence for the gods of Old that he became able to discern their forms by starlight as they strode, unseen by others, among men. Each night did Shaun discern the forms of the gods and every day he taught concerning them, till men in Averon knew how the gods appeared all grey against the mountains, and how Rhoog was higher than Mount Scagadon, and how Skun was smaller, and how Asgool leaned forward as he strode, and how Trodath peered about him with small eyes. But one night as Shaun watched the gods of Old by starlight, he faintly discerned some other gods that sat far up the slopes of the mountains in the stillness behind the gods of Old. And the next day he hurled his robe away that he wore as Averon's prophet and said to his people:

"There be gods greater than the gods of Old, three gods seen faintly on the hills by starlight looking on Averon."

And Shaun set out and travelled many days and many people followed him. And every night he saw more clearly the shapes of the three new gods who sat silent when the gods of Old were striding among men. On the higher slopes of the mountain Shaun stopped with all his people, and there they built a city and worshipped the gods, whom only Shaun could see, seated above them on the mountain. And Shaun taught how the gods were like grey streaks of light seen before dawn, and how the god on the right pointed upward toward the sky, and how the god on the left pointed downward toward the ground, but the god in the middle slept.

And in the city Shaun's followers built three temples. The one on the right was a temple for the young, and the one on the left a temple for the old, and the third was a temple for the old, and the third was a temple with doors closed and barred—therein none ever entered. One night as Shaun watched before the three gods sitting like pale light against the mountain, he saw on the mountain's summit two gods that spake together and pointed, mocking the gods of the hill, only he heard no sound. The next day Shaun set out and a few followed him to climb to the mountain's summit in the cold, to find the gods who were so great that they mocked at the silent three. And near the two gods they halted and built for themselves huts. Also they built a temple wherein the Two were carved by the hand of Shaun with their heads turned towards each other, with mockery on Their faces and Their fingers pointing, and beneath Them were carved the three gods of the hill as actors making sport. None remembered now Asgool, Trodath, Skun, and Rhoog, the gods of Old.

36

Time and the Gods

For many years Shaun and his few followers lived in their huts upon the mountain's summit worshipping gods that mocked, and every night Shaun saw the two gods by starlight as they laughed to one another in the silence. And Shaun grew old.

One night as his eyes were turned towards the Two, he saw across the mountains in the distance a great god seated in the plain and looming enormous to the sky, who looked with angry eyes towards the Two as they sat and mocked. Then said Shaun to his people, the few that had followed him thither:

"Alas that we may not rest, but beyond us in the plain sitteth the one true god and he is wroth with mocking. Let us therefore leave these two that sit and mock and let us find the truth in the worship of that greater god, who even though he kill shall yet not mock us."

But the people answered:

"Thou hast taken from us many gods and taught us now to worship gods that mock, and if there is laughter on their faces as we die, lo! thou alone canst see it, and we would rest."

But three men who had grown old with following followed still.

And down the steep mountain on the further side Shaun led them, saying:

"Now we shall surely know."

And the three old men answered:

"We shall know indeed, O last of all the prophets."

That night the two gods mocking at their worshippers mocked not at Shaun nor his three followers, who coming to the plain still travelled on till they came at last to a place where the eyes of Shaun at night could closely see the vast form of their god. And beyond them as far as the sky there lay a marsh. There they rested, building such shelters as they could, and said to one another:

"This is the End, for Shaun discerneth that there are no more gods, and before us lieth the marsh and old age hath come upon us."

Time and the Gods

And since they could not labour to build a temple, Shaun carved upon a rock all that he saw by starlight of the great god of the plain; so that if ever others forsook the gods of Old because they saw beyond them the Greater Three, and should thence come to knowledge of the Twain that mocked, and should yet persevere in wisdom till they saw by starlight him whom Shaun named the Ultimate god, they should still find there upon the rock what one had written concerning the end of search. For three years Shaun carved upon the rock, and rising one night from carving, saying:

"Now is my labour done," saw in the distance four greater gods beyond the Ultimate god. Proudly in the distance beyond the marsh these gods were tramping together, taking no heed of the god upon the plain. Then said Shaun to his three followers:

"Alas that we know not yet, for there be gods beyond the marsh."

None would follow Shaun, for they said that old age must end all quests, and that they would rather wait there in the plain for Death than that he should pursue them across the marsh.

Then Shaun said farewell to his followers, saying:

"You have followed me well since ever we forsook the gods of Old to worship greater gods. Farewell. It may be that your prayers at evening shall avail when you pray to the god of the plain, but I must go onward, for there be gods beyond."

So Shaun went down into the marsh, and for three days struggled through it, and on the third night saw the four gods not very far away, yet could not discern Their faces. All the next day Shaun toiled on to see Their faces by starlight, but ere the night came up or one star shone, at set of sun, Shaun fell down before the feet of his four gods. The stars came out, and the faces of the four shone bright and clear, but Shaun saw them not, for the labour of toiling and seeing was over for Shaun; and lo! They were Asgool, Trodath, Skun, and Rhoog—The gods of Old.

Then said the King:

"It is well that the sorrow of search cometh only to the wise, for the wise are very few."

Also the King said:

"Tell me this thing, O prophet. Who are the true gods?"

The master prophet answered:

"Let the King command."

THE MEN OF YARNITH

The men of Yarnith hold that nothing began until Yarni Zai uplifted his hand. Yarni Zai, they say, has the form of a man but is greater and is a thing of rock. When he uplifted his hand all the rocks that wandered beneath the Dome, by which name they call the sky, gathered together around Yarni Zai.

Of the other worlds they say nought, but hold that the stars are the eyes of all the other gods that look on Yarni Zai and laugh, for they are all greater than he, though they have gathered no worlds around them.

Yet though they be greater than Yarni Zai, and though they laugh at him when they speak together beneath the Dome, they all speak of Yarni Zai.

Unheard is the speaking of the gods to all except the gods, but the men of Yarnith tell of how their prophet Iraun lying in the sand desert, Azrakhan, heard once their speaking and knew thereby how Yarni Zai departed from all the other gods to clothe himself with rocks and make a world.

Certain it is that every legend tells that at the end of the valley of Yodeth, where it becomes lost among black cliffs, there sits a figure colossal, against a mountain, whose form is the form of a man with the right hand uplifted, but vaster than the hills. And in the Book of Secret Things which the prophets keep in the Temple that stands in Yarnith is writ the story of the gathering of the world as Iraun heard it when the gods spake together, up in the stillness above Azrakhan.

And all that read this may learn how Yarni Zai drew the mountains about him like a

39

cloak, and piled the world below him. It is not set in writing for how many years Yarni Zai sat clothed with rocks at the end of the Valley of Yodeth, while there was nought in all the world save rocks and Yarni Zai.

But one day there came another god running over the rocks across the world, and he ran as the clouds run upon days of storm, and as he sped towards Yodeth, Yarni Zai, sitting against his mountain with right hand uplifted, cried out:

"What dost thou, running across my world, and whither art thou going?"

And the new god answered never a word, but sped onwards, and as he went to left of him and to right of him there sprang up green things all over the rocks of the world of Yarni Zai.

So the new god ran round the world and made it green, saying in the valley where Yarni Zai sat monstrous against his mountain and certain lands wherein Cradoa, the drought, browsed horribly at night.

Further, the writing in the book tells of how there came yet another god running speedily out of the east, as swiftly as the first, with his face set westward, and nought to stay his running; and how he stretched both arms outward beside him, and to left of him and to right of him as he ran the whole world whitened.

And Yarni Zai called out:

"What dost thou, running across my world?"

And the new god answered:

"I bring the snow for all the world—whiteness and resting and stillness."

And he stilled the running of streams and laid his hand even upon the head of Yarni Zai and muffled the noises of the world, till there was no sound in all lands, but the running of the new god that brought the snow as he sped across the plains.

Time and the Gods

But the two new gods chased each other for ever round the world, and every year they passed again, running down the valleys and up the hills and away across the plains before Yarni Zai, whose hand uplifted had gathered the world about him.

And, furthermore, the very devout may read how all the animals came up the valley of Yodeth to the mountain whereon rested Yarni Zai, saying:

"Give us leave to live, to be lions, rhinoceroses and rabbits, and to go about the world."

And Yarni Zai gave leave to the animals to be lions, rhinoceroses and rabbits, and all the other kinds of beasts, and to go about the world. But when they all had gone he gave leave to the bird to be a bird and to go about the sky.

And further there came a man into that valley who said:

"Yarni Zai, thou hast made animals into thy world. O Yarni Zai, ordain that there be men."

So Yarni Zai made men.

Then was there in the world Yarni Zai, and two strange gods that brought the greenness and the growing and the whiteness and the stillness, and animals and men.

And the god of the greenness pursued the god of the whiteness, and the god of the whiteness pursued the god of the greenness, and men pursued animals, and animals pursued men. But Yarni Zai sat still against his mountain with his right hand uplifted. But the men of Yarnith say that when the arm of Yarni Zai shall cease to be uplifted the world shall be flung behind him, as a man's cloak is flung away. And Yarni Zai, no longer clad with the world, shall go back into the emptiness beneath the Dome among the stars, as a diver seeking pearls goes down from the islands.

It is writ in Yarnith's histories by scribes of old that there passed a year over the valley of Yarnith that bore not with it any rain; and the Famine from the wastes beyond, finding that it was dry and pleasant in Yarnith, crept over the mountains and down their slopes and sunned himself at the edge of Yarnith's fields.

Time and the Gods

And men of Yarnith, labouring in the fields, found the Famine as he nibbled at the corn and chased the cattle, and hastily they drew water from deep wells and cast it over the Famine's dry grey fur and drove him back to the mountains. But the next day when his fur was dry again the Famine returned and nibbled more of the corn and chased the cattle further, and again men drove him back. But again the Famine returned, and there came a time when there was no more water in the wells to frighten the Famine with, and he nibbled the corn till all of it was gone and the cattle that he chased grew very lean. And the Famine drew nearer, even to the houses of men and trampled on their gardens at night and ever came creeping nearer to their doors. At last the cattle were able to run no more, and one by one the Famine took them by their throats and dragged them down, and at night he scratched in the ground, killing even the roots of things, and came and peered in at the doorways and started back and peered in at the door again a little further, but yet was not bold enough to enter altogether, for fear that men should have water to throw over his dry grey fur.

Then did the men of Yarnith pray to Yarni Zai as he sat far off beyond the valley, praying to him night and day to call his Famine back, but the Famine sat and purred and slew all the cattle and dared at last to take men for his food.

And the histories tell how he slew children first and afterwards grew bolder and tore down women, till at last he even sprang at the throats of men as they laboured in the fields.

Then said the men of Yarnith:

"There must go one to take our prayers to the feet of Yarni Zai; for the world at evening utters many prayers, and it may be that Yarni Zai, as he hears all earth lamenting when the prayers at evening flutter to his feet, may have missed among so many the prayers of the men of Yarnith. But if one go and say to Yarni Zai: 'There is a little crease in the outer skirts of thy cloak that men call the valley of Yarnith, where the Famine is a greater lord than Yarni Zai,' it may be that he shall remember for an instant and call his Famine back."

Yet all men feared to go, seeing that they were but men and Yarni Zai was Lord of the whole earth, and the journey was far and rocky. But that night Hothrun Dath heard the Famine whining outside his house and pawing at his door; therefore, it seemed to him more meet to wither before the glance of Yarni Zai than that the whining of that Famine should ever again fall upon his ears.

So about the dawn, Hothrun Dath crept away, fearing still to hear behind him the breathing of the Famine, and set out upon his journey whither pointed the graves of men. For men in Yarnith are buried with their feet and faces turned toward Yarni Zai, lest he might beckon to them in their night and call them to him.

So all day long did Hothrun Dath follow the way of the graves. It is told that he even journeyed for three days and nights with nought but the graves to guide him, as they pointed towards Yarni Zai where all the world slopes upwards towards Yodeth, and the great black rocks that are nearest to Yarni Zai lie gathered together by clans, till he came to the two great black pillars of asdarinth and saw the rocks beyond them piled in a dark valley, narrow and aloof, and knew that this was Yodeth. Then did he haste no more, but walked quietly up the valley, daring not to disturb the stillness, for he said:

"Surely this is the stillness of Yarni Zai, which lay about him before he clothed himself with rocks."

Here among the rocks which first had gathered to the call of Yarni Zai, Hothrun Dath felt a mighty fear, but yet went onwards because of all his people and because he knew that thrice in every hour in some dark chamber Death and Famine met to speak two words together, "The End."

But as dawn turned the darkness into grey, he came to the valley's end, and even touched the foot of Yarni Zai, but saw him not, for he was all hidden in the mist. Then Hothrun Dath feared that he might not behold him to look him in the eyes when he sent up his prayer. But laying his forehead against the foot of Yarni Zai he prayed for the men of Yarnith, saying:

"O Lord of Famine and Father of Death, there is a spot in the world that thou hast cast about thee which men call Yarnith, and there men die before the time thou hast apportioned, passing out of Yarnith. Perchance the Famine hath rebelled against thee, or Death exceeds his powers. O Master of the World, drive out the Famine as a moth out of thy cloak, lest the gods beyond that regard thee with their eyes say—there is Yarni Zai, and lo! his cloak is tattered."

Time and the Gods

And in the mist no sign made Yarni Zai. Then did Hothrun Dath pray to Yarni Zai to make some sign with his uplifted hand that he might know he heard him. In the awe and silence he waited, until nigh the dawn the mist that hid the figure rolled upwards. Serene above the mountains he brooded over the world, silent, with right hand uplifted.

What Hothrun Dath saw there upon the face of Yarni Zai no history telleth, or how he came again alive to Yarnith, but this is writ that he fled, and none hath since beheld the face of Yarni Zai. Some say that he saw a look on the face of the image that set a horror tingling through his soul, but it is held in Yarnith that he found the marks of instruments of carving about the figure's feet, and discerning thereby that Yarni Zai was wrought by the hands of men, he fled down the valley screaming:

"There are no gods, and all the world is lost." And hope departed from him and all the purposes of life. Motionless behind him, lit by the rising sun, sat the colossal figure with right hand uplifted that man had made in his own image.

But the men of Yarnith tell how Hothrun Dath came back again panting to his own city, and told the people that there were no gods and that Yarnith had no hope from Yarni Zai. Then the men of Yarnith when they knew that the Famine came not from the gods, arose and strove against him. They dug deep for wells, and slew goats for food high up on Yarnith's mountains and went afar and gathered blades of grass, where yet it grew, that their cattle might live. Thus they fought the Famine, for they said: "If Yarni Zai be not a god, then is there nothing mightier in Yarnith than men, and who is the Famine that he should bare his teeth against the lords of Yarnith?"

And they said: "If no help cometh from Yarni Zai then is there no help but from our own strength and might, and we be Yarnith's gods with the saving of Yarnith burning within us or its doom according to our desire."

And some more the Famine slew, but others raised their hands saying: "These be the hands of gods," and drave the Famine back till he went from the houses of men and out among the cattle, and still the men of Yarnith pursued him, till above the heat of the fight came the million whispers of rain heard faintly far off towards evening. Then the Famine fled away howling back to the mountains and over the mountains' crests, and became no more than a thing that is told in Yarnith's legends.

Time and the Gods

A thousand years have passed across the graves of those that fell in Yarnith by the Famine. But the men of Yarnith still pray to Yarni Zai, carved by men's hands in the likeness of a man, for they say—"It may be that the prayers we offer to Yarni Zai may roll upwards from his image as do the mists at dawn, and somewhere find at last the other gods or that God who sits behind the others of whom our prophets know not."

FOR THE HONOUR OF THE GODS

Of the great wars of the Three Islands are many histories writ and of how the heroes of the olden time one by one were slain, but nought is told of the days before the olden time, or ever the people of the isles went forth to war, when each in his own land tended cattle or sheep, and listless peace obscured those isles in the days before the olden time. For then the people of the Islands played like children about the feet of Chance and had no gods and went not forth to war. But sailors, cast by strange winds upon those shores which they named the Prosperous Isles, and finding a happy people which had no gods, told how they should be happier still and know the gods and fight for the honour of the gods and leave their names writ large in histories and at the last die proclaiming the names of the gods. And the people of the islands met and said:

"The beasts we know, but lo! these sailors tell of things beyond that know us as we know the beasts and use us for their pleasure as we use the beasts, but yet are apt to answer idle prayer flung up at evening near the hearth, when a man returneth from the ploughing of the fields. Shall we now seek these gods?" And some said:

"We are lords of the Three Islands and have none to trouble us, and while we live we find prosperity, and when we die our bones have ease in the quiet. Let us not therefore seek those who may loom greater than we do in the Islands Three or haply harry our bones when we be dead."

But others said:

"The prayers that a man mutters, when the drought hath come and all the cattle die, go up unheeded to the heedless clouds, and if somewhere there be those that garner prayer let us send men to seek them and to say: 'There be men in the Isles called Three, or sometimes named by sailors the Prosperous Isles (and they be in the Central Sea), who ofttimes pray,

45

and it hath been told us that ye love the worship of men, and for it answer prayer, and we be travellers from the Islands Three.'"

And the people of the Islands were greatly allured by the thought of strange things neither men nor beasts who at evening answered prayer.

Therefore they sent men down in ships with sails to sail across the sea, and in safety over the sea to a far shore Chance brought the ships. Then over hill and valley three men set forth seeking to find the gods, and their comrades beached the ships and waited on the shore. And they that sought the gods followed for thirty nights the lightnings in the sky over five mountains, and as they came to the summit of the last, they saw a valley beneath them, and lo! the gods. For there the gods sat, each on a marble hill, each sitting with an elbow on his knee, and his chin upon his hand, and all the gods were smiling about Their lips. And below them there were armies of little men, and about the feet of the gods they fought against each other and slew one another for the honour of the gods, and for the glory of the name of the gods. And round them in the valley their cities that they had builded with the toil of their hands, they burned for the honour of the gods, where they died for the honour of the gods, and the gods looked down and smiled. And up from the valley fluttered the prayers of men and here and there the gods did answer a prayer, but oftentimes They mocked them, and all the while men died.

And they that had sought the gods from the Islands Three, having seen what they had seen, lay down on the mountain summit lest the gods should see them. Then they crept backward a little space, still lying down, and whispered together and then stooped low and ran, and travelled across the mountains in twenty days and came again to their comrades by the shore. But their comrades asked them if their quest had failed and the three men only answered:

"We have seen the gods."

And setting sail the ships hove back across the Central Sea and came again to the Islands Three, where rest the feet of Chance, and said to the people:

"We have seen the gods."

Time and the Gods

But to the rulers of the Islands they told how the gods drove men in herds; and went back and tended their flocks again all in the Prosperous Isles, and were kinder to their cattle after they had seen how that the gods used men.

But the gods walking large about Their valley, and peering over the great mountain's rim, saw one morning the tracks of the three men. Then the gods bent their faces low over the tracks and leaning forward ran, and came before the evening of the day to the shore where the men had set sail in ships, and saw the tracks of ships upon the sand, and waded far out into the sea, and yet saw nought. Still it had been well for the Islands Three had not certain men that had heard the travellers' tale sought also to see the gods themselves. These in the night-time slipped away from the Isles in ships, and ere the gods had retreated to the hills, They saw where ocean meets with sky the full white sails of those that sought the gods upon an evil day. Then for a while the people of those gods had rest while the gods lurked behind the mountain, waiting for the travellers from the Prosperous Isles. But the travellers came to shore and beached their ships, and sent six of their number to the mountain whereof they had been told. But they after many days returned, having not seen the gods but only the smoke that went upward from burned cities, and vultures that stood in the sky instead of answered prayer. And they all ran down their ships again into the sea, and set sail again and came to the Prosperous Isles. But in the distance crouching behind the ships the gods came wading through the sea that They might have the worship of the isles. And to every isle of the three the gods showed themselves in different garb and guise, and to all they said:

"Leave your flocks. Go forth and fight for the honour of the gods."

And from one of the isles all the folk came forth in ships to battle for gods that strode through the isle like kings. And from another they came to fight for gods that walked like humble men upon the earth in beggars' rags; and the people of the other isle fought for the honour of gods that were clothed in hair like beasts; and had many gleaming eyes and claws upon their foreheads. But of how these people fought till the isles grew desolate but very glorious, and all for the fame of the gods, are many histories writ.

NIGHT AND MORNING

Once in an arbour of the gods above the fields of twilight Night wandering alone came suddenly on Morning. Then Night drew from his face his cloak of dark grey mists and said: "See, I am Night," and they two sitting in that arbour of the gods, Night told wondrous stories of old mysterious happenings in the dark. And Morning sat and wondered, gazing into the face of Night and at his wreath of stars. And Morning told how the rains of Snamarthis smoked in the plain, but Night told how Snamarthis held riot in the dark, with revelry and drinking and tales told by kings, till all the hosts of Meenath crept against it and the lights went out and there arose the din of arms or ever Morning came. And Night told how Sindana the beggar had dreamed that he was a King, and Morning told how she had seen Sindana find suddenly an army in the plain, and how he had gone to it thinking he was King and the army had believed him, and Sindana now ruled over Marthis and Targadrides, Dynath, Zahn, and Tumeida. And most Night loved to tell of Assarnees, whose ruins are scant memories on the desert's edge, but Morning told of the twin cities of Nardis and Timaut that lorded over the plain. And Night told terribly of what Mynandes found when he walked through his own city in the dark. And ever at the elbow of regal Night whispers arose saying: "Tell Morning *this*."

And ever Night told and ever Morning wondered. And Night spake on, and told what the dead had done when they came in the darkness on the King that had led them into battle once. And Night knew who slew Darnex and how it was done. Moreover, he told why the seven Kings tortured Sydatheris and what Sydatheris said just at the last, and how the Kings went forth and took their lives.

And Night told whose blood had stained the marble steps that lead to the temple in Ozahn, and why the skull within it wears a golden crown, and whose soul is in the wolf that howls in the dark against the city. And Night knew whither the tigers go out of the Irasian desert and the place where they meet together, and who speaks to them and what she says and why. And he told why human teeth had bitten the iron hinge in the great gate that swings in the walls of Mondas, and who came up out of the marsh alone in the darktime and demanded audience of the King and told the King a lie, and how the King, believing it, went down into the vaults of his palace and found only toads and snakes, who slew the King. And he told of ventures in palace towers in the quiet, and knew the spell whereby a man might send the light of the moon right into the soul of his foe. And Night spoke of the forest and the stirring of shadows and soft feet pattering and peering eyes, and of the fear that sits behind the trees taking to itself the shape of something crouched to spring.

But far under that arbour of the gods down on the earth the mountain peak Mondana looked Morning in the eyes and forsook his allegiance to Night, and one by one the lesser hills about Mondana's knees greeted the Morning. And all the while in the plains the shapes of cities came looming out of the dusk. And Kongros stood forth with all her pinnacles, and the winged figure of Poesy carved upon the eastern portal of her gate, and the squat figure of Avarice carved facing it upon the west; and the bat began to tire of going up and down her streets, and already the owl was home. And the dark lions went up out of the plain back to their caves again. Not as yet shone any dew upon the spider's snare nor came the sound of any insects stirring or bird of the day, and full allegiance all the valleys owned still to their Lord the Night. Yet earth was preparing for another ruler, and kingdom by kingdom she stole away from Night, and there marched through the dreams of men a million heralds that cried with the voice of the cock: "Lo! Morning come behind us." But in that arbour of the gods above the fields of twilight the star wreath was paling about the head of Night, and ever more wonderful on Morning's brow appeared the mark of power. And at the moment when the camp fires pale and the smoke goes grey to the sky, and camels sniff the dawn, suddenly Morning forgot Night. And out of that arbour of the gods, and away to the haunts of the dark, Night with his swart cloak slunk away; and Morning placed her hand upon the mists and drew them upward and revealed the earth, and drove the shadows before her, and they followed Night. And suddenly the mystery quitted haunting shapes, and an old glamour was gone, and far and wide over the fields of earth a new splendour arose.

USURY

The men of Zonu hold that Yahn is God, who sits as a usurer behind a heap of little lustrous gems and ever clutches at them with both his arms. Scarce larger than a drop of water are the gleaming jewels that lie under the grasping talons of Yahn, and every jewel is a life. Men tell in Zonu that the earth was empty when Yahn devised his plan, and on it no life stirred. Then Yahn lured to him shadows whose home was beyond the Rim, who knew little of joys and nought of any sorrow, whose place was beyond the Rim before the birth of Time. These Yahn lured to him and showed them his heap of gems; and in the jewels there was light, and green fields glistened in them, and there were glimpses of blue sky and little streams, and very faintly little gardens showed that flowered in orchard lands. And some showed winds in the heaven, and some showed the arch of the sky with a waste plain drawn across it, with grasses bent in the wind and never aught but the plain.

But the gems that changed the most had in their centre the ever changing sea. Then the shadows gazed into the Lives and saw the green fields and the sea and earth and the gardens of earth. And Yahn said: "I will loan you each a Life, and you may do your work with it upon the Scheme of Things, and have each a shadow for his servant in green fields and in gardens, only for these things you shall polish these Lives with experience and cut their edges with your griefs, and in the end shall return them again to me."

And thereto the shadows consented, that they might have gleaming Lives and have shadows for their servants, and this thing became the Law. But the shadows, each with his Life, departed and came to Zonu and to other lands, and there with experience they polished the Lives of Yahn, and cut them with human griefs until they gleamed anew. And ever they found new scenes to gleam within these Lives, and cities and sails and men shone in them where there had been before only green fields and sea, and ever Yahn the usurer cried out to remind them of their bargain. When men added to their Lives scenes that were pleasant to Yahn, then was Yahn silent, but when they added scenes that pleased not the eyes of Yahn, then did he take a toll of sorrow from them because it was the Law.

But men forgot the usurer, and there arose some claiming to be wise in the Law, who said that after their labour, which they wrought upon their Lives, was done, those Lives should be theirs to possess; so men took comfort from their toil and labour and the grinding and cutting of their griefs. But as their Lives began to shine with experience of many things, the thumb and forefinger of Yahn would suddenly close upon a Life, and the man became a shadow. But away beyond the Rim the shadows say:

"We have greatly laboured for Yahn, and have gathered griefs in the world, and caused his Lives to shine, and Yahn doeth nought for us. Far better had we stayed where no cares are, floating beyond the Rim."

And there the shadows fear lest ever again they be lured by specious promises to suffer usury at the hands of Yahn, who is overskilled in Law. Only Yahn sits and smiles, watching his hoard increase in preciousness, and hath no pity for the poor shadows whom he hath lured from their quiet to toil in the form of men.

And ever Yahn lures more shadows and sends them to brighten his Lives, sending the old Lives out again to make them brighter still; and sometimes he gives to a shadow a Life that was once a king's and sendeth him with it down to the earth to play the part of a beggar, or sometimes he sendeth a beggar's Life to play the part of a king. What careth Yahn?

The men of Zonu have been promised by those that claim to be wise in the Law that their Lives which they have toiled at shall be theirs to possess for ever, yet the men of Zonu fear that Yahn is greater and overskilled in the Law. Moreover it hath been said that Time will bring the hour when the wealth of Yahn shall be such as his dreams have lusted for. Then shall Yahn leave the earth at rest and trouble the shadows no more, but sit and gloat with his unseemly face over his hoard of Lives, for his soul is a usurer's soul. But others say, and they swear that this is true, that there are gods of Old, who be far greater than Yahn, who made the Law wherein Yahn is overskilled, and who will one day drive a bargain with him that shall be too hard for Yahn. Then Yahn shall wander away, a mean forgotten god, and perchance in some forsaken land shall haggle with the rain for a drop of water to drink, for his soul is a usurer's soul. And the Lives—who knoweth the gods of Old or what Their will shall be?

MLIDEEN

Upon an evening of the forgotten years the gods were seated upon Mowrah Nawut above Mlideen holding the avalanche in leash.

All in the Middle City stood the Temples of the city's priests, and hither came all the people of Mlideen to bring them gifts, and there it was the wont of the City's priests to carve them gods for Mlideen. For in a room apart in the Temple of Eld in the midst of the temples that stood in the Middle City of Mlideen there lay a book called the Book of Beautiful Devices, writ in a language that no man may read and writ long ago, telling how a man may make for himself gods that shall neither rage nor seek revenge against a little people. And ever the priests came forth from reading in the Book of Beautiful Devices and ever they sought to make benignant gods, and all the gods that they made were different from each other, only their eyes turned all upon Mlideen.

But upon Mowrah Nawut for all of the forgotten years the gods had waited and forborne until the people of Mlideen should have carven one hundred gods. Never came lightnings from Mowrah Nawut crashing upon Mlideen, nor blight on harvests nor pestilence in the

51

city, only upon Mowrah Nawut the gods sat and smiled. The people of Mlideen had said: "Yoma is god." And the gods sat and smiled. And after the forgetting of Yoma and the passing of years the people had said: "Zungari is god." And the gods sat and smiled.

Then on the altar of Zungari a priest had set a figure squat, carven in purple agate, saying: "Yazun is god." Still the gods sat and smiled.

About the feet of Yonu, Bazun, Nidish and Sundrao had gone the worship of the people of Mlideen, and still the gods sat holding the avalanche in leash above the city.

There set a great calm towards sunset over the heights, and Mowrah Nawut stood up still with gleaming snow, and into the hot city cool breezes blew from his benignant slopes as Tarsi Zalo, high prophet of Mlideen, carved out of a great sapphire the city's hundredth god, and then upon Mowrah Nawut the gods turned away saying: "One hundred infamies have now been wrought." And they looked no longer upon Mlideen and held the avalanche no more in leash, and he leapt forward howling.

Over the Middle City of Mlideen now lies a mass of rocks, and on the rocks a new city is builded wherein people dwell who know not old Mlideen, and the gods are seated on Mowrah Nawut still. And in the new city men worship carven gods, and the number of the gods that they have carven is ninety and nine, and I, the prophet, have found a curious stone and go to carve it into the likeness of a god for all Mlideen to worship.

THE SECRET OF THE GODS

Zyni Moe, the small snake, saw the cool river gleaming before him afar off and set out over the burning sand to reach it.

Uldoon, the prophet, came out of the desert and followed up the bank of the river towards his old home. Thirty years since Uldoon had left the city, where he was born, to live his life in a silent place where he might search for the secret of the gods. The name of his home was the City by the River, and in that city many prophets taught concerning many gods, and men made many secrets for themselves, but all the while none knew the Secret of the gods. Nor might any seek to find it, for if any sought men said of him:

Time and the Gods

"This man sins, for he giveth no worship to the gods that speak to our prophets by starlight when none heareth."

And Uldoon perceived that the mind of a man is as a garden, and that his thoughts are as the flowers, and the prophets of a man's city are as many gardeners who weed and trim, and who have made in the garden paths both smooth and straight, and only along these paths is a man's soul permitted to go lest the gardeners say, "This soul transgresseth." And from the paths the gardeners weed out every flower that grows, and in the garden they cut off all flowers that grow tall, saying:

"It is customary," and "it is written," and "this hath ever been," or "that hath not been before."

Therefore Uldoon saw that not in that city might he discover the Secret of the gods. And Uldoon said to the people:

"When the worlds began, the Secret of the gods lay written clear over the whole earth, but the feet of many prophets have trampled it out. Your prophets are all true men, but I go into the desert to find a truth which is truer than your prophets." Therefore Uldoon went into the desert and in storm and still he sought for many years. When the thunder roared over the mountains that limited the desert he sought the Secret in the thunder, but the gods spake not by the thunder. When the voices of the beasts disturbed the stillness under the stars he sought the secret there, but the gods spake not by the beasts.

Uldoon grew old and all the voices of the desert had spoken to Uldoon, but not the gods, when one night he heard Them whispering beyond the hills. And the gods whispered one to another, and turning Their faces earthward They all wept. And Uldoon though he saw not the gods yet saw Their shadows turn as They went back to a great hollow in the hills; and there, all standing in the valley's mouth, They said:

"Oh, Morning Zai, oh, oldest of the gods, the faith of thee is gone, and yesterday for the last time thy name was spoken upon earth." And turning earthward they all wept again. And the gods tore white clouds out of the sky and draped them about the body of Morning Zai and bore him forth from his valley behind the hills, and muffled the mountain peaks with snow, and beat upon their summits with drum sticks carved of ebony, playing the dirge of the gods. And the echoes rolled about the passes and the winds howled, because the faith of the olden days was gone, and with it had sped the soul of Morning Zai. So through the mountain passes the gods came at night bearing Their dead father. And Uldoon followed. And the gods came to a great sepulchre of onyx that stood upon four fluted pillars of white marble, each carved out of four mountains, and therein the gods laid Morning Zai because the old faith was fallen. And there at the tomb of Their father the gods spake and Uldoon heard the Secret of the gods, and it became to him a simple thing such as a man might well guess—yet hath not. Then the soul of the desert arose and cast over the tomb its wreath of forgetfulness devised of drifting sand, and the gods strode home across the mountains to Their hollow land. But Uldoon left the desert and travelled many days, and so came to the river where it passes beyond the city to seek the sea, and following its bank came near to his old home. And the people of the City by the River, seeing him far off, cried out:

"Hast thou found the Secret of the gods?"

And he answered:

"I have found it, and the Secret of the gods is this"—:

Zyni Moe, the small snake, seeing the figure and the shadow of a man between him and the cool river, raised his head and struck once. And the gods are pleased with Zyni Moe, and have called him the protector of the Secret of the gods.

THE SOUTH WIND

Two players sat down to play a game together to while eternity away, and they chose the gods as pieces wherewith to play their game, and for their board of playing they chose the sky from rim to rim, whereon lay a little dust; and every speck of dust was a world upon the board of playing. And the players were robed and their faces veiled, and the robes and veils were alike, and their names were Fate and Chance. And as they played their game and moved the gods hither and thither about the board, the dust arose, and shone in the light from the players' eyes that gleamed behind the veils. Then said the gods: "See how We stir the dust."

It chanced, or was ordained (who knoweth which?) that Ord, a prophet, one night saw the

54

gods as They strode knee deep among the stars. But as he gave Them worship, he saw the hand of a player, enormous over Their heads, stretched out to make his move. Then Ord, the prophet, knew. Had he been silent it might have still been well with Ord, but Ord went about the world crying out to all men, "There is a power over the gods."

This the gods heard. Then said They, "Ord hath seen."

Terrible is the vengeance of the gods, and fierce were Their eyes when They looked on the head of Ord and snatched out of his mind all knowledge of Themselves. And that man's soul went wandering afield to find for itself gods, for ever finding them not. Then out of Ord's Dream of Life the gods plucked the moon and the stars, and in the night–time he only saw black sky and saw the lights no more. Next the gods took from him, for Their vengeance resteth not, the birds and butterflies, flowers and leaves and insects and all small things, and the prophet looked on the world that was strangely altered, yet knew not of the anger of the gods. Then the gods sent away his familiar hills, to be seen no more by him, and all the pleasant woodlands on their summits and the further fields; and in a narrower world Ord walked round and round, now seeing little, and his soul still wandered searching for some gods and finding none.

Lastly, the gods took away the fields and stream and left to the prophet only his house and the larger things that were in it. Day by day They crept about him drawing films of mist between him and familiar things, till at last he beheld nought at all and was quite blind and unaware of the anger of the gods. Then Ord's world became only a world of sound, and only by hearing he kept his hold upon Things. All the profit that he had out of his days was here some song from the hills or there the voice of the birds, and sound of the stream, or the drip of the falling rain. But the anger of the gods ceases not with the closing of flowers, nor is it assuaged by all the winter's snows, nor doth it rest in the full glare of summer, and They snatched away from Ord one night his world of sound and he awoke deaf. But as a man may smite away the hive of the bee, and the bee with all his fellows builds again, knowing not what hath smitten his hive or that it shall smite again, so Ord built for himself a world out of old memories and set it in the past. There he builded himself cities out of former joys, and therein built palaces of mighty things achieved, and with his memory as a key he opened golden locks and had still a world to live in, though the gods had taken from him the world of sound and all the world of sight. But the gods tire not from pursuing, and They seized his world of former things and took his memory away and covered up the paths that led into the past, and left him blind and deaf and forgetful among men, and caused all men to know that this was he who once had said that the gods were little things.

And lastly the gods took his soul, and out of it They fashioned the South Wind to roam the seas for ever and not have rest; and well the South Wind knows that he hath once understood somewhere and long ago, and so he moans to the islands and cries along southern shores, "I have known," and "I have known."

But all things sleep when the South Wind speaks to them and none heed his cry that he hath known, but are rather content to sleep. But still the South Wind, knowing that there is something that he hath forgot, goes on crying, "I have known," seeking to urge men to arise and to discover it. But none heed the sorrows of the South Wind even when he driveth his tears out of the South, so that though the South Wind cries on and on and never findeth rest none heed that there is aught that may be known, and the Secret of the gods is safe. But the business of the South Wind is with the North, and it is said that the time will one day come when he shall overcome the bergs and sink the seas of ice and come where the Secret of the gods is graven upon the pole. And the game of Fate and Chance shall suddenly cease and He that loses shall cease to be or ever to have been, and from the board of playing Fate or Chance (who knoweth which shall win?) shall sweep the gods away.

IN THE LAND OF TIME

Thus Karnith, King of Alatta, spake to his eldest son: "I bequeath to thee my city of Zoon, with its golden eaves, whereunder hum the bees. And I bequeath to thee also the land of Alatta, and all such other lands as thou art worthy to possess, for my three strong armies which I leave thee may well take Zindara and over-run Istahn, and drive back Onin from his frontier, and leaguer the walls of Yan, and beyond that spread conquest over the lesser lands of Hebith, Ebnon, and Karida. Only lead not thine armies against Zeenar, nor ever cross the Eidis."

Thereat in the city of Zoon in the land of Alatta, under his golden eaves, died King Karnith, and his soul went whither had gone the souls of his sires the elder Kings, and the souls of their slaves.

Time and the Gods

Then Karnith Zo, the new King, took the iron crown of Alatta and afterwards went down to the plains that encircle Zoon and found his three strong armies clamouring to be led against Zeenar, over the river Eidis.

But the new King came back from his armies, and all one night in the great palace alone with his iron crown, pondered long upon war; and a little before dawn he saw dimly through his palace window, facing east over the city of Zoon and across the fields of Alatta, to far off where a valley opened on Istahn. There, as he pondered, he saw the smoke arising tall and straight over small houses in the plain and the fields where the sheep fed. Later the sun rose shining over Alatta as it shone over Istahn, and there arose a stir about the houses both in Alatta and Istahn, and cocks crowded in the city and men went out into the fields among the bleating sheep; and the King wondered if men did otherwise in Istahn. And men and women met as they went out to work and the sound of laughter arose from streets and fields; the King's eyes gazed into the distance toward Istahn and still the smoke went upward tall and straight from the small houses. And the sun rose higher that shone upon Alatta and Istahn, causing the flowers to open wide in each, and the birds to sing and the voices of men and women to arise. And in the market place of Zoon caravans were astir that set out to carry merchandise to Istahn, and afterwards passed camels coming to Alatta with many tinkling bells. All this the King saw as he pondered much, who had not pondered before. Westward the Agnid mountains frowned in the distance guarding the river Eidis; behind them the fierce people of Zeenar lived in a bleak land.

Later the King, going abroad through his new kingdom, came on the Temple of the gods of Old. There he found the roof shattered and the marble columns broken and tall weeds met together in the inner shrine, and the gods of Old, bereft of worship or sacrifice, neglected and forgotten. And the King asked of his councillors who it was that had overturned this temple of the gods or caused the gods Themselves to be thus forsaken. And they answered him:

"Time has done this."

Next the King came upon a man bent and crippled, whose face was furrowed and worn, and the King having seen no such sight within the court of his father said to the man:

"Who hath done this thing to you?"

57

Time and the Gods

And the old man answered:

"Time hath ruthlessly done it."

But the King and his councillors went on, and next they came upon a body of men carrying among them a hearse. And the King asked his councillors closely concerning death, for these things had not before been expounded to the King. And the oldest of the councillors answered:

"Death, O King, is a gift sent by the gods by the hand of their servant Time, and some receive it gladly, and some are forced reluctantly to take it, and before others it is suddenly flung in the middle of the day. And with this gift that Time hath brought him from the gods a man must go forth into the dark to possess no other thing for so long as the gods are willing."

But the King went back to his palace and gathered the greatest of his prophets and his councillors and asked them more particularly concerning Time. And they told the King how that Time was a great figure standing like a tall shadow in the dusk or striding, unseen, across the world, and how that he was the slave of the gods and did Their bidding, but ever chose new masters, and how all the former masters of Time were dead and Their shrines forgotten. And one said:

"I have seen him once when I went down to play again in the garden of my childhood because of certain memories. And it was towards evening and the light was pale, and I saw Time standing over the little gate, pale like the light, and he stood between me and that garden and had stolen my memories because he was mightier than I."

And another said:

"I, too, have seen the Enemy of my House. For I saw him when he strode over the fields that I knew well and led a stranger by the hand to place him in my home to sit where my forefathers sat. And I saw him afterwards walk thrice round the house and stoop and gather up the glamour from the lawns and brush aside the tall poppies in the garden and spread weeds in his pathway where he strode through the remembered nooks."

And another said:

Time and the Gods

"He went one day into the desert and brought up life out of the waste places, and made it cry bitterly and covered it with the desert again."

And another said:

"I too saw him once seated in the garden of a child tearing the flowers, and afterwards he went away through many woodlands and stooped down as he went, and picked the leaves one by one from the trees."

And another said:

"I saw him once by moonlight standing tall and black amidst the ruins of a shrine in the old kingdom of Amarna, doing a deed by night. And he wore a look on his face such as murderers wear as he busied himself to cover over something with weeds and dust. Thereafter in Amarna the people of that old Kingdom missed their god, in whose shrine I saw Time crouching in the night, and they have not since beheld him."

And all the while from the distance at the city's edge rose a hum from the three armies of the King clamouring to be led against Zeenar. Thereat the King went down to his three armies and speaking to their chiefs said:

"I will not go down clad with murder to be King over other lands. I have seen the same morning arising on Istahn that also gladdened Alatta, and have heard Peace lowing among the flowers. I will not desolate homes to rule over an orphaned land and a land widowed. But I will lead you against the pledged enemy of Alatta who shall crumble the towers of Zoon and hath gone far to overthrow our gods. He is the foe of Zindara and Istahn and many–citadeled Yan, Hebith and Ebnon may not overcome him nor Karida be safe against him among her bleakest mountains. He is a foe mightier than Zeenar with frontiers stronger than Eidis; he leers at all the peoples of the earth and mocks their gods and covets their builded cities. Therefore we will go forth and conquer Time and save the gods of Alatta from his clutch, and coming back victorious shall find that Death is gone and age and illness departed, and here we shall live for ever by the golden eaves of Zoon, while the bees hum among unrusted gables and never crumbling towers. There shall be neither fading nor forgetting, nor ever dying nor sorrow, when we shall have freed the people and pleasant fields of the earth from inexorable Time."

59

Time and the Gods

And the armies swore that they would follow the King to save the world and the gods.

So the next day the King set forth with his three armies and crossed many rivers and marched through many lands, and wherever they went they asked for news of Time.

And the first day they met a woman with her face furrowed and lined, who told them that she had been beautiful and that Time had smitten her in the face with his five claws.

Many an old man they met as they marched in search of Time. All had seen him but none could tell them more, except that some said he went that way and pointed to a ruined tower or to an old and broken tree.

And day after day and month by month the King pushed on with his armies, hoping to come at last on Time. Sometimes they encamped at night near palaces of beautiful design or beside gardens of flowers, hoping to find their enemy when he came to desecrate in the dark. Sometimes they came on cobwebs, sometimes on rusted chains and houses with broken roofs or crumbling walls. Then the armies would push on apace thinking that they were closer upon the track of Time.

As the weeks passed by and weeks grew to months, and always they heard reports and rumours of Time, but never found him, the armies grew weary of the great march, but the King pushed on and would let none turn back, saying always that the enemy was near at hand.

Month in, month out, the King led on his now unwilling armies, till at last they had marched for close upon a year and came to the village of Astarma very far to the north. There many of the King's weary soldiers deserted from his armies and settled down in Astarma and married Astarmian girls. By these soldiers we have the march of the armies clearly chronicled to the time when they came to Astarma, having been nigh a year upon the march. And the army left that village and the children cheered them as they went up the street, and five miles distant they passed over a ridge of hills and out of sight. Beyond this less is known, but the rest of this chronicle is gathered from the tales that the veterans of the King's armies used to tell in the evenings about the fires in Zoon and remembered afterwards by the men of Zeenar.

Time and the Gods

It is mostly credited in these days that such of the King's armies as went on past Astarma came at last (it is not known after how long a time) over a crest of a slope where the whole earth slanted green to the north. Below it lay green fields and beyond them moaned the sea with never shore nor island so far as the eye could reach. Among the green fields lay a village, and on this village the eyes of the King and his armies were turned as they came down the slope. It lay beneath them, grave with seared antiquity, with old-world gables stained and bent by the lapse of frequent years, with all its chimneys awry. Its roofs were tiled with antique stones covered over deep with moss, each little window looked with a myriad strange cut panes on the gardens shaped with quaint devices and overrun with weeds. On rusted hinges the doors sung to and fro and were fashioned of planks of immemorial oak with black knots gaping from their sockets. Against it all there beat the thistle-down, about it clambered the ivy or swayed the weeds; tall and straight out of the twisted chimneys arose blue columns of smoke, and blades of grass peeped upward between the huge cobbles of the unmolested street. Between the gardens and the cobbled streets stood hedges higher than a horseman might look, of stalwart thorn, and upward through it clambered the convolvulus to peer into the garden from the top. Before each house there was cut a gap in the hedge, and in it swung a wicket gate of timber soft with the rain and years, and green like the moss. Over all of it there brooded age and the full hush of things bygone and forgotten. Upon this derelict that the years had cast up out of antiquity the King and his armies gazed long. Then on the hill slope the King made his armies halt, and went down alone with one of his chiefs into the village.

Presently there was a stir in one of the houses, and a bat flew out of the door into the daylight, and three mice came running out of the doorway down the step, an old stone cracked in two and held together by moss; and there followed an old man bending on a stick with a white beard coming to the ground, wearing clothes that were glossed with use, and presently there came others out of the other houses, all of them as old, and all hobbling on sticks. These were the oldest people that the King had ever beheld, and he asked them the name of the village and who they were; and one of them answered, "This is the City of the Aged in the Territory of Time."

And the King said, "Is Time then here?"

And one of the old men pointed to a great castle standing on a steep hill and said: "Therein dwells Time, and we are his people;" and they all looked curiously at King Karnith Zo, and the eldest of the villagers spoke again and said: "Whence do you come, you that are so young?" and Karnith Zo told him how he had come to conquer Time to save the world and the gods, and asked them whence they came.

And the villagers said:

"We are older than always, and know not whence we came, but we are the people of Time, and here from the Edge of Everything he sends out his hours to assail the world, and you may never conquer Time." But the King went back to his armies, and pointed towards the castle on the hill and told them that at last they had found the Enemy of the Earth; and they that were older than always went back slowly into their houses with the creaking of olden doors. And there they went across the fields and passed the village. From one of his towers Time eyed them all the while, and in battle order they closed in on the steep hill as Time sat still in his great tower and watched.

But as the feet of the foremost touched the edge of the hill Time hurled five years against them, and the years passed over their heads and the army still came on, an army of older men. But the slope seemed steeper to the King and to every man in his army, and they breathed more heavily. And Time summoned up more years, and one by one he hurled them at Karnith Zo and at all his men. And the knees of the army stiffened, and their beards grew and turned grey, and the hours and days and the months went singing over their heads, and their hair turned whiter and whiter, and the conquering hours bore down, and the years rushed on and swept the youth of that army clear away till they came face to face under the walls of the castle of Time with a mass of howling years, and found the top of the slope too steep for aged men. Slowly and painfully, harassed with agues and chills, the King rallied his aged army that tottered down the slope.

Slowly the King led back his warriors over whose heads had shrieked the triumphant years. Year in, year out, they straggled southwards, always towards Zoon; they came, with rust upon their spears and long beards flowing, again into Astarma, and none knew them there. They passed again by towns and villages where once they had inquired curiously concerning Time, and none knew them there either. They came again to the palaces and gardens where they had waited for Time in the night, and found that Time had been there. And all the while they set a hope before them that they should come on Zoon again and see its golden eaves. And no one knew that unperceived behind them there lurked and followed the gaunt figure of Time cutting off stragglers one by one and overwhelming them with his hours, only men were missed from the army every day, and fewer and fewer grew the veterans of Karnith Zo.

But at last after many a month, one night as they marched in the dusk before the morning, dawn suddenly ascending shone on the eaves of Zoon, and a great cry ran through the army:

"Alatta, Alatta!"

But drawing nearer they found that the gates were rusted and weeds grew tall along the outer walls, many a roof had fallen, gables were blackened and bent, and the golden eaves shone not as heretofore. And the soldiers entering the city expecting to find their sisters and sweethearts of a few years ago saw only old women wrinkled with great age and knew not who they were.

Suddenly someone said:

"He has been here too."

And then they knew that while they searched for Time, Time had gone forth against their city and leaguered it with the years, and had taken it while they were far away and enslaved their women and children with the yoke of age. So all that remained of the three armies of Karnith Zo settled in the conquered city. And presently the men of Zeenar crossed over the river Eidis and easily conquering an army of aged men took all Alatta for themselves, and their kings reigned thereafter in the city of Zoon. And sometimes the men of Zeenar listened to the strange tales that the old Alattans told of the years when they made battle against Time. Such of these tales as the men of Zeenar remembered they afterwards set forth, and this is all that may be told of those adventurous armies that went to war with Time to save the world and the gods, and were overwhelmed by the hours and the years.

THE RELENTING OF SARNIDAC

The lame boy Sarnidac tended sheep on a hill to the southward of the city. Sarnidac was a dwarf and greatly derided in the city. For the women said:

Time and the Gods

"It is very funny that Sarnidac is a dwarf," and they would point their fingers at him saying:—"This is Sarnidac, he is a dwarf; also he is very lame."

Once the doors of all the temples in the world swung open to the morning, and Sarnidac with his sheep upon the hill saw strange figures going down the white road, always southwards. All the morning he saw the dust rising above the strange figures and always they went southwards right as far as the rim of the Nydoon hills where the white road could be seen no more. And the figures stooped and seemed to be larger than men, but all men seemed very large to Sarnidac, and he could not see clearly through the dust. And Sarnidac shouted to them, as he hailed all people that passed down the long white road, and none of the figures looked to left or right and none of them turned to answer Sarnidac. But then few people ever answered him because he was lame, and a small dwarf.

Still the figures went striding swiftly, stooping forward through the dust, till at last Sarnidac came running down his hill to watch them closer. As he came to the white road the last of the figures passed him, and Sarnidac ran limping behind him down the road.

For Sarnidac was weary of the city wherein all derided him, and when he saw these figures all hurrying away he thought that they went perhaps to some other city beyond the hills over which the sun shone brighter, or where there was more food, for he was poor, even perhaps where people had not the custom of laughing at Sarnidac. So this procession of figures that stooped and seemed larger than men went southward down the road and a lame dwarf hobbled behind them.

Khamazan, now called the City of the Last of Temples, lies southward of the Nydoon hills. This is the story of Pompeides, now chief prophet of the only temple in the world, and greatest of all the prophets that have been:

On the slopes of Nydoon I was seated once above Khamazan. There I saw figures in the morning striding through much dust along the road that leads across the world. Striding up the hill they came towards me, not with the gait of men, and soon the first one came to the crest of the hill where the road dips to find the plains again, where lies Khamazan. And now I swear by all the gods that are gone that this thing happened as I shall say it, and was surely so. When those that came striding up the hill came to its summit they took not the road that goes down into the plains nor trod the dust any longer, but went straight

64

Time and the Gods

on and upwards, striding as they strode before, as though the hill had not ended nor the road dipped. And they strode as though they trod no yielding substance, yet they stepped upwards through the air.

This the gods did, for They were not born men who strode that day so strangely away from earth.

But I, when I saw this thing, when already three had passed me, leaving earth, cried out before the fourth:

'Gods of my childhood, guardians of little homes, whither are ye going, leaving the round earth to swim alone and forgotten in so great a waste of sky?'

And one answered:

'Heresy apace shoots her fierce glare over the world and men's faith grows dim and the gods go. Men shall make iron gods and gods of steel when the wind and the ivy meet within the shrines of the temples of the gods of old.'

And I left that place as a man leaves fire by night, and going plainwards down the white road that the gods spurned cried out to all that I passed to follow me, and so crying came to the city's gates. And there I shouted to all near the gates:

'From yonder hilltop the gods are leaving earth.'

Then I gathered many, and we all hastened to the hill to pray the gods to tarry, and there we cried out to the last of the departing gods:

'Gods of old prophecy and of men's hopes, leave not the earth, and all our worship shall hum about Your ears as never it hath before, and oft the sacrifice shall squeal upon Your altars.'

And I said:—

'Gods of still evenings and quiet nights, go not from earth and leave not Your carven shrines, and all men shall worship You still. For between us and yonder still blue spaces

65

oft roam the thunder and the storms, there in his hiding lurks the dark eclipse, and there are stored all snows and hails and lightnings that shall vex the earth for a million years. Gods of our hopes, how shall men's prayers crying from empty shrines pass through such terrible spaces; how shall they ever fare above the thunder and many storms to whatever place the gods may go in that blue waste beyond?'

But the gods bent straight forward, and trampled through the sky and looked not to the right nor left nor downwards, nor ever heeded my prayer.

And one cried out hoping yet to stay the gods, though nearly all were gone, saying:—

'O gods, rob not the earth of the dim hush that hangs round all Your temples, bereave not all the world of old romance, take not the glamour from the moonlight nor tear the wonder out of the white mists in every land; for, O ye gods of the childhood of the world, when You have left the earth you shall have taken the mystery from the sea and all its glory from antiquity, and You shall have wrenched out hope from the dim future. There shall be no strange cries at night time half understood, nor songs in the twilight, and the whole of the wonder shall have died with last year's flowers in little gardens or hill–slopes leaning south; for with the gods must go the enchantment of the plains and all the magic of dark woods, and something shall be lacking from the quiet of early dawn. For it would scarce befit the gods to leave the earth and not take with Them that which They had given it. Out beyond the still blue spaces Ye will need the holiness of sunset for Yourselves and little sacred memories and the thrill that is in stories told by firesides long ago. One strain of music, one song, one line of poetry and one kiss, and a memory of one pool with rushes, and each one the best, shall the gods take to whom the best belongs, when the gods go.

'Sing a lamentation, people of Khamazan, sing a lamentation for all the children of earth at the feet of the departing gods. Sing a lamentation for the children of earth who now must carry their prayers to empty shrines and around empty shrines must rest at last.'

Then when our prayers were ended and our tears shed, we beheld the last and smallest of the gods halted upon the hilltop. Twice he called to Them with a cry somewhat like the cry wherewith our shepherds hail their brethren, and long gazed after Them, and then deigned to look no longer and to tarry upon earth and turn his eyes on men. Then a great shout went up when we saw that our hopes were saved and that there was still on earth a

66

haven for our prayers. Smaller than men now seemed the figures that had loomed so big, as one behind the other far over our heads They still strode upwards. But the small god that had pitied the world came with us down the hill, still deigning to tread the road, though strangely, not as men tread, and into Khamazan. There we housed him in the palace of the King, for that was before the building of the temple of gold, and the King made sacrifice before him with his own hands, and he that had pitied the world did eat the flesh of the sacrifice.

And the Book of the Knowledge of the gods in Khamazan tells how the small god that pitied the world told his prophets that his name was Sarnidac and that he herded sheep, and that therefore he is called the shepherd god, and sheep are sacrificed upon his altars thrice a day, and the North, East, West and the South are the four hurdles of Sarnidac and the white clouds are his sheep. And the Book of the Knowledge of the gods tells further how the day on which Pompeides found the gods shall be kept for ever as a fast until the evening and called the Fast of the Departing, but in the evening shall a feast be held which is named the Feast of the Relenting, for on that evening Sarnidac pitied the whole world and tarried.

And the people of Khamazan all prayed to Sarnidac, and dreamed their dreams and hoped their hopes because their temple was not empty. Whether the gods that are departed be greater than Sarnidac none know in Khamazan, but some believe that in their azure windows They have set lights that lost prayers swarming upwards may come to them like moths and at last find haven and light far up above the evening and the stillness where sit the gods.

But Sarnidac wondered at the strange figures, at the people of Khamazan, and at the palace of the King and the customs of the prophets, but wondered not more greatly at aught in Khamazan than he had wondered at the city which he had left. For Sarnidac, who had not known why men were unkind to him, thought that he had found at last the land for which the gods had let him hope, where men should have the custom of being kind to Sarnidac.

THE JEST OF THE GODS

Once the Older gods had need of laughter. Therefore They made the soul of a king, and set in it ambitions greater than kings should have, and lust for territories beyond the lust of other kings, and in this soul They set strength beyond the strength of others and fierce desire for power and a strong pride. Then the gods pointed earthward and sent that soul into the fields of men to live in the body of a slave. And the slave grew, and the pride and lust for power began to arise in his heart, and he wore shackles on his arms. Then in the Fields of Twilight the gods prepared to laugh.

But the slave went down to the shore of the great sea, and cast his body away and the shackles that were upon it, and strode back to the Fields of Twilight and stood up before the gods and looked Them in Their faces. This thing the gods, when They had prepared to laugh, had not foreseen. Lust for power burned strong in that King's soul, and there was all the strength and pride in it that the gods had placed therein, and he was too strong for the Older gods. He whose body had borne the lashes of men could brook no longer the dominion of the gods, and standing before Them he bade the gods to go. Up to Their lips leapt all the anger of the Older gods, being for the first time commanded, but the King's soul faced Them still, and Their anger died away and They averted Their eyes. Then Their thrones became empty, and the Fields of Twilight bare as the gods slunk far away. But the soul chose new companions.

THE DREAMS OF THE PROPHET

I

When the gods drave me forth to toil and assailed me with thirst and beat me down with hunger, then I prayed to the gods. When the gods smote the cities wherein I dwelt, and when Their anger scorched me and Their eyes burned, then did I praise the gods and offer sacrifice. But when I came again to my green land and found that all was gone, and the old mysterious haunts wherein I prayed as a child were gone, and when the gods tore up the dust and even the spider's web from the last remembered nook, then did I curse the gods, speaking it to Their faces, saying:—

"Gods of my prayers! Gods of my sacrifice! because Ye have forgotten the sacred places of my childhood, and they have therefore ceased to be, yet may I not forget. Because Ye have done this thing, Ye shall see cold altars and shall lack both my fear and praise. I shall not wince at Your lightnings, nor be awed when Ye go by."

Time and the Gods

Then looking seawards I stood and cursed the gods, and at this moment there came to me one in the garb of a poet, who said:—

"Curse not the gods."

And I said to him:

"Wherefore should I not curse Those that have stolen my sacred places in the night, and trodden down the gardens of my childhood?"

And he said "Come, and I will show thee." And I followed him to where two camels stood with their faces towards the desert. And we set out and I travelled with him for a great space, he speaking never a word, and so we came at last to a waste valley hid in the desert's midst. And herein, like fallen moons, I saw vast ribs that stood up white out of the sand, higher than the hills of the desert. And here and there lay the enormous shapes of skulls like the white marble domes of palaces built for tyrannous kings a long while since by armies of driven slaves. Also there lay in the desert other bones, the bones of vast legs and arms, against which the desert, like a besieging sea, ever advanced and already had half drowned. And as I gazed in wonder at these colossal things the poet said to me:

"The gods are dead."

And I gazed long in silence, and I said:

"These fingers, that are now so dead and so very white and still, tore once the flowers in gardens of my youth."

But my companion said to me:

"I have brought thee here to ask of thee thy forgiveness of the gods, for I, being a poet, knew the gods, and would fain drive off the curses that hover above Their bones and bring Them men's forgiveness as an offering at the last, that the weeds and the ivy may cover Their bones from the sun."

And I said:

Time and the Gods

"They made Remorse with his fur grey like a rainy evening in the autumn, with many rending claws, and Pain with his hot hands and lingering feet, and Fear like a rat with two cold teeth carved each out of the ice of either pole, and Anger with the swift flight of the dragonfly in summer having burning eyes. I will not forgive these gods."

But the poet said:

"Canst thou be angry with these beautiful white bones?" And I looked long at those curved and beautiful bones that were no longer able to hurt the smallest creature in all the worlds that they had made. And I thought long of the evil that they had done, and also of the good. But when I thought of Their great hands coming red and wet from battles to make a primrose for a child to pick, then I forgave the gods.

And a gentle rain came falling out of heaven and stilled the restless sand, and a soft green moss grew suddenly and covered the bones till they looked like strange green hills, and I heard a cry and awoke and found that I had dreamed, and looking out of my house into the street I found that a flash of lightning had killed a child. Then I knew that the gods still lived.

II

I lay asleep in the poppy fields of the gods in the valley of Alderon, where the gods come by night to meet together in council when the moon is low. And I dreamed that this was the Secret.

Fate and Chance had played their game and ended, and all was over, all the hopes and tears, regrets, desires and sorrows, things that men wept for and unremembered things, and kingdoms and little gardens and the sea, and the worlds and the moons and the suns; and what remained was nothing, having neither colour nor sound.

Then said Fate to Chance: "Let us play our old game again." And they played it again together, using the gods as pieces, as they had played it oft before. So that those things which have been shall all be again, and under the same bank in the same land a sudden glare of singlight on the same spring day shall bring the same daffodil to bloom once more and the same child shall pick it, and not regretted shall be the billion years that fell between. And the same old faces shall be seen again, yet not bereaved of their familiar

70

haunts. And you and I shall in a garden meet again upon an afternoon in summer when the sun stands midway between his zenith and the sea, where we met oft before. For Fate and Chance play but one game together with every move the same, and they play it oft to while eternity away.

PART II. THE JOURNEY OF THE KING

I

One day the King turned to the women that danced and said to them: "Dance no more," and those that bore the wine in jewelled cups he sent away. The palace of King Ebalon was emptied of sound of song and there rose the voices of heralds crying in the streets to find the prophets of the land.

Then went the dancers, the cupbearer and the singers down into the hard streets among the houses, Pattering Leaves, Silvern Fountain and Summer Lightning, the dancers whose feet the gods had not devised for stony ways, which had only danced for princes. And with them went the singer, Soul of the South, and the sweet singer, Dream of the Sea, whose voices the gods had attuned to the ears of kings, and old Istahn the cupbearer left his life's work in the palace to tread the common ways, he that had stood at the elbows of three kings of Zarkandhu and had watched his ancient vintage feeding their valour and mirth as the waters of Tondaris feed the green plains to the south. Ever he had stood grave among their jests, but his heart warmed itself solely by the fire of the mirth of Kings. He too, with the singers and dancers, went out into the dark.

And throughout the land the heralds sought out the prophets thereof. Then one evening as King Ebalon sat alone within his palace there were brought before him all who had repute for wisdom and who wrote the histories of the times to be. Then the King spake, saying: "The King goeth upon a journey with many horses, yet riding upon none, when the pomp of travelling shall be heard in the streets and the sound of the lute and the drum and the name of the King. And I would know what princes and what people shall greet me on the other shore in the land to which I travel."

Then fell a hush upon the prophets for they murmured: "All knowledge is with the King."

Time and the Gods

Then said the King: "Thou first, Samahn, High Prophet of the Temple of gold in Azinorn, answer or thou shalt write no more the history of the times to be, but shalt toil with thy hand to make record of the little happenings of the days that were, as do the common men."

Then said Samahn: "All knowledge is with the King," and when the pomp of travelling shall be heard in the streets and the slow horses whereon the King rideth not go behind lute and drum, then, as the King well knoweth, thou shalt go down to the great white house of Kings and, entering the portals where none are worthy to follow, shalt make obeisance alone to all the elder Kings of Zarkandhu, whose bones are seated upon golden thrones grasping their sceptres still. Therein thou shalt go with robes and sceptre through the marble porch, but thou shalt leave behind thee thy gleaming crown that others may wear it, and as the times go by come in to swell the number of the thirty Kings that sit in the great white house on golden thrones. There is one doorway in the great white house, and it stands wide with marble portals yawning for kings, but when it shall receive thee, and thine obeisance hath been made because of thine obligation to the thirty Kings, thou shalt find at the back of the house an unknown door through which the soul of a King may just pass, and leaving thy bones upon a golden throne thou shalt go unseen out of the great white house to tread the velvet spaces that lie among the worlds. Then, O King, it were well to travel fast and not to tarry about the houses of men as do the souls of some who still bewail the sudden murder that sent them upon the journey before their time, and who, being yet both to go, linger in dark chambers all the night. These, setting forth to travel in the dawn and travelling all the day, see earth behind them gleaming when an evening falls, and again are loth to leave its pleasant haunts, and come back again through dark woods and up into some old loved chamber, and ever tarry between home and flight and find no rest.

Thou wilt set forth at once because the journey is far and lasts for many hours; but the hours on the velvet spaces are the hours of the gods, and we may not say what time such an hour may be if reckoned in mortal years.

At last thou shalt come to a grey place filled with mist, with grey shapes standing before it which are altars, and on the altars rise small red flames from dying fires that scarce illumine the mist. And in the mist it is dark and cold because the fires are low. These are the altars of the people's faiths, and the flames are the worship of men, and through the mist the gods of Old go groping in the dark and in the cold. There thou shalt hear a voice

72

cry feebly: "Inyani, Inyani, lord of the thunder, where art thou, for I cannot see?" And a voice shall answer faintly in the cold: "O maker of many worlds, I am here." And in that place the gods of Old are nearly deaf for the prayers of men grow few, they are nigh blind because the fires burn low upon the altars of men's faiths and they are very cold. And all about the place of mist there lies a moaning sea which is called the Sea of Souls. And behind the place of mist are the dim shapes of mountains, and on the peak of one there glows a silvern light that shines in the moaning sea; and ever as the flames on the altars die before the gods of Old the light on the mountain increases, and the light shines over the mist and never through it as the gods of Old grow blind. It is said that the light on the mountain shall one day become a new god who is not of the gods of Old.

There, O King, thou shalt enter the Sea of Souls by the shore where the altars stand which are covered in mist. In that sea are the souls of all that ever lived on the worlds and all that ever shall live, all freed from earth and flesh. And all the souls in that sea are aware of one another but more than with hearing or sight or by taste or touch or smell, and they all speak to each other yet not with lips, with voices which need no sound. And over the sea lies music as winds o'er an ocean on earth, and there unfettered by language great thoughts set outward through the souls as on earth the currents go.

Once did I dream that in a mist–built ship I sailed upon that sea and heard the music that is not of instruments, and voices not from lips, and woke and found that I was upon the earth and that the gods had lied to me in the night. Into this sea from fields of battle and cities come down the rivers of lives, and ever the gods have taken onyx cups and far and wide into the worlds again have flung the souls out of the sea, that each soul may find a prison in the body of a man with five small windows closely barred, and each one shackled with forgetfulness.

But all the while the light on the mountain grows, and none may say what work the god that shall be born of the silvern light shall work on the Sea of Souls, when the gods of Old are dead and the Sea is living still.

And answer made the King:

"Thou that art a prophet of the gods of Old, go back and see that those red flames burn more brightly on the altars in the mist, for the gods of Old are easy and pleasant gods, and thou canst not say what toil shall vex our souls when the god of the light on the mountain shall stride along the shore where bleach the huge bones of the gods of Old."

And Samahn answered: "All knowledge is with the King."

II

Then the King called to Ynath bidding him speak concerning the journey of the King. Ynath was the prophet that sat at the Eastern gate of the Temple of Gorandhu. There Ynath prayed his prayers to all the passers by lest ever the gods should go abroad, and one should pass him dressed in mortal guise. And men are pleased as they walk by that Eastern gate that Ynath should pray to them for fear that they be gods, so men bring gifts to Ynath in the Eastern gate.

And Ynath said: "All knowledge is with the King. When a strange ship comes to anchor in the air outside thy chamber window, thou shalt leave thy well–kept garden and it shall become a prey to the nights and days and be covered again with grass. But going aboard thou shalt set sail over the Sea of Time and well shall the ship steer through the many worlds and still sail on. If other ships shall pass thee on the way and hail thee saying: 'From what port' thou shalt answer them: 'From Earth.' And if they ask thee 'whither bound?' then thou shalt answer: 'The End.' Or thou shalt hail them saying: 'From what port?' And they shall answer: 'From The End called also The Beginning, and bound to Earth.' And thou shalt sail away till like an old sorrow dimly felt by happy men the worlds shall gleam in the distance like one star, and as the star pales thou shalt come to the shore of space where aeons rolling shorewards from Time's sea shall lash up centuries to foam away in years. There lies the Centre Garden of the gods, facing full seawards. All around lie songs that on earth were never sung, fair thoughts not heard among the worlds, dream pictures never seen that drifted over Time without a home till at last the aeons swept them on to the shore of space. And in the Centre Garden of the gods bloom many fancies. Therein once some souls were playing where the gods walked up and down and to and fro. And a dream came in more beauteous than the rest on the crest of a wave of Time, and one soul going downward to the shore clutched at the dream and caught it. Then over the dreams and stories and old songs that lay on the shore of space the hours came sweeping back, and the centuries caught that soul and swirled him with his dream far out to the Sea of Time, and the aeons swept him earthwards and cast him into a palace with all the might of the sea and left him there with his dream. The child grew to a King

74

and still clutched at his dream till the people wondered and laughed. Then, O King, Thou didst cast thy dream back into the Sea, and Time drowned it and men laughed no more, but thou didst forget that a certain sea beat on a distant shore and that there was a garden and therein souls. But at the end of the journey that thou shalt take, when thou comest to the shore of space again thou shalt go up the beach, and coming to a garden gate that stands in a garden wall shalt remember these things again, for it stands where the hours assail not above the beating of Time, far up the shore, and nothing altereth there. So thou shalt go through the garden gate and hear again the whispering of the souls when they talk low where sing the voices of the gods. There with kindred souls thou shalt speak as thou didst of yore and tell them what befell thee beyond the tides of time and how they took thee and made of thee a King so that thy soul found no rest. There in the Centre Garden thou shalt sit at ease and watch the gods all rainbow–clad go up and down and to and fro on the paths of dreams and songs, and shalt not venture down to the cheerless sea. For that which a man loves most is not on this side of Time, and all which drifts on its aeons is a lure.

"All knowledge is with the King."

Then said the King: "Ay, there was a dream once but Time hath swept it away."

III

Then spake Monith, Prophet of the Temple of Azure that stands on the snow–peak of Ahmoon and said: "All knowledge is with the King. Once thou didst set out upon a one day's journey riding thy horse and before thee had gone a beggar down the road, and his name was Yeb. Him thou didst overtake and when he heeded not thy coming thou didst ride over him.

"Upon the journey that thou shalt one day take riding upon no horse, this beggar has set out before thee and is labouring up the crystal steps towards the moon as a man goeth up the steps of a high tower in the dark. On the moon's edge beneath the shadow of Mount Angises he shall rest awhile and then shall climb the crystal steps again. Then a great journey lies before him before he may rest again till he come to that star that is called the left eye of Gundo. Then a journey of many crystal steps lieth before him again with nought to guide him but the light of Omrazu. On the edge of Omrazu shall Yeb tarry long, for the most dreadful part of his journey lieth before him. Up the crystal steps that lie beyond Omrazu he must go, and any that follow, though the howling of all the meteors that ride the sky; for in that part of the crystal space go many meteors up and down all squealing in the dark, which greatly perplex all travellers. And, if he may see though the gleaming of the meteors and in spite of their uproar come safely through, he shall come to the star Omrund at the edge of the Track of Stars. And from star to star along the Track of Stars the soul of a man may travel with more ease, and there the journey lies no more straight forward, but curves to the right."

Then said King Ebalon:

"Of this beggar whom my horse smote down thou hast spoken much, but I sought to know by what road a King should go when he taketh his last royal journey, and what princes and what people should meet him upon another shore."

Then answered Monith:

"All knowledge is with the King. It hath been doomed by the gods, who speak not in jest, that thou shalt follow the soul that thou didst send alone upon its journey, that that soul go not unattended up the crystal steps.

"Moreover, as this beggar went upon his lonely journey he dared to curse the King, and his curses lie like a red mist along the valleys and hollows wherever he uttered them. By these red mists, O King, thou shalt track him as a man follows a river by night until thou shalt fare at last to the land wherein he hath blessed thee (repenting of anger at last), and thou shalt see his blessing lie over the land like a blaze of golden sunshine illumining fields and gardens."

Then said the King:

"The gods have spoken hard above the snowy peak of this mountain Ahmoon."

And Monith said:

"How a man may come to the shore of space beyond the tides of time I know not, but it is doomed that thou shalt certainly first follow the beggar past the moon, Omrund and

Time and the Gods

Omrazu till thou comest to the Track of Stars, and up the Track of Stars coming towards the right along the edge of it till thou comest to Ingazi. There the soul of the beggar Yeb sat long, then, breathing deep, set off on his great journey earthward adown the crystal steps. Straight through the spaces where no stars are found to rest at, following the dull gleam of earth and her fields till he come at last where journeys end and start."

Then said King Ebalon:

"If this hard tale be true, how shall I find the beggar that I must follow when I come again to the earth?"

And the Prophet answered:

"Thou shalt know him by his name and find him in this place, for that beggar shall be called King Ebalon and he shall be sitting upon the throne of the Kings of Zarkandhu."

And the King answered:

"If one sit upon this throne whom men call King Ebalon, who then shall I be?"

And the Prophet answered:

"Thou shalt be a beggar and thy name shall be Yeb, and thou shalt ever tread the road before the palace waiting for alms from the King whom men shall call Ebalon."

Then said the King:

"Hard gods indeed are those that tramp the snows of Ahmoon about the temple of Azure, for if I sinned against this beggar called Yeb, they too have sinned against him when they doomed him to travel on this weary journey though he hath not offended."

And Monith said:

"He too hath offended, for he was angry as thy horse struck him, and the gods smite anger. And his anger and his curses doom him to journey without rest as also they doom thee."

Time and the Gods

Then said the King:

"Thou that sittest upon Ahmoon in the Temple of Azure, dreaming thy dreams and making prophecies, foresee the ending of this weary quest and tell me where it shall be?"

And Monith answered:

"As a man looks across great lakes I have gazed into the days to be, and as the great flies come upon four wings of gauze to skim over blue waters, so have my dreams come sailing two by two out of the days to be. And I dreamed that King Ebalon, whose soul was not thy soul, stood in his palace in a time far hence, and beggars thronged the street outside, and among them was Yeb, a beggar, having thy soul. And it was on the morning of a festival and the King came robed in white, with all his prophets and his seers and magicians, all down the marble steps to bless the land and all that stood therein as far as the purple hills, because it was the morning of festival. And as the King raised up his hand over the beggars' heads to bless the fields and rivers and all that stood therein, I dreamed that the quest was ended.

"All knowledge is with the King."

IV

Evening darkened and above the palace domes gleamed out the stars whereon haply others missed the secret too.

And outside the palace in the dark they that had borne the wine in jewelled cups mocked in low voices at the King and at the wisdom of his prophets.

Then spake Ynar, called the prophet of the Crystal Peak; for there rises Amanath above all that land, a mountain whose peak is crystal, and Ynar beneath its summit hath his Temple, and when day shines no longer on the world Amanath takes the sunlight and gleams afar as a beacon in a bleak land lit at night. And at the hour when all faces are turned on Amanath, Ynar comes forth beneath the Crystal peak to weave strange spells and to make signs that people say are surely for the gods. Therefore it is said in all those lands that Ynar speaks at evening to the gods when all the world is still.

Time and the Gods

And Ynar said:

"All knowledge is with the King, and without doubt it hath come to the King's ears how certain speech is held at evening on the Peak of Amanath.

"They that speak to me at evening on the Peak are They that live in a city through whose streets Death walketh not, and I have heard it from Their Elders that the King shall take no journey; only from thee the hills shall slip away, the dark woods, the sky and all the gleaming worlds that fill the night, and the green fields shall go on untrodden by thy feet and the blue sky ungazed at by thine eyes, and still the rivers shall all run seaward but making no music in thine ears. And all the old laments shall still be spoken, troubling thee not, and to the earth shall fall the tears of the children of earth and never grieving thee. Pestilence, heat and cold, ignorance, famine and anger, these things shall grip their claws upon all men as heretofore in fields and roads and cities but shall not hold thee. But from thy soul, sitting in the old worn track of the worlds when all is gone away, shall fall off the shackles of circumstance and thou shalt dream thy dreams alone.

"And thou shalt find that dreams are real where there is nought as far as the Rim but only thy dreams and thee.

"With them thou shalt build palaces and cities resting upon nothing and having no place in time, not to be assailed by the hours or harmed by ivy or rust, not to be taken by conquerors, but destroyed by thy fancy if thou dost wish it so or by thy fancy rebuilded. And nought shall ever disturb these dreams of thine which here are troubled and lost by all the happenings of earth, as the dreams of one who sleeps in a tumultuous city. For these thy dreams shall sweep outward like a strong river over a great waste plain wherein are neither rocks nor hills to turn it, only in that place there shall be no boundaries nor sea, neither hindrance nor end. And it were well for thee that thou shouldst take few regrets into thy waste dominions from the world wherein thou livest, for such regrets or any memory of deeds ill done must sit beside thy soul forever in that waste, singing one song always of forlorn remorse; and they too shall be only dreams but very real.

"There nought shall hinder thee among thy dreams, for even the gods may harass thee no more when flesh and earth and events with which They bound thee shall have slipped away."

Time and the Gods

Then said the King:

"I like not this grey doom, for dreams are empty. I would see action roaring through the world, and men and deeds."

Then answered the Prophet:

"Victory, jewels and dancing but please thy fancy. What is the sparkle of the gem to thee without thy fancy which it allures, and thy fancy is all a dream. Action and deeds and men are nought without dreams and do but fetter them, and only dreams are real, and where thou stayest when the worlds shall drift away there shall be only dreams."

And the King answered:

"A mad prophet."

And Ynar said:

"A mad prophet, but believing that his soul possesseth all things of which his soul may become aware and that he is master of that soul, and thou a high–minded King believing only that thy soul possesseth such few countries as are leaguered by thine armies and the sea, and that thy soul is possessed by certain strange gods of whom thou knowest not, who shall deal with it in a way whereof thou knowest not. Until a knowledge come to us that either is wrong I have wider realms, I King, than thee and hold them beneath no overlords."

Then said the King:

"Thou hast said no overlords! To whom then dost thou speak by strange signs at evening above the world?"

And Ynar went forward and whispered to the King. And the King shouted:

"Seize ye this prophet for he is a hypocrite and speaks to no gods at evening above the world, but has deceived us with his signs."

Time and the Gods

And Ynar said:

"Come not near me or I shall point towards you when I speak at evening upon the mountain with Those that ye know of."

Then Ynar went away and the guards touched him not.

V

Then spake the prophet Thun, who was clad in seaweed and had no Temple, but lived apart from men. All his life he had lived on a lonely beach and had heard for ever the wailing of the sea and the crying of the wind in hollows among the cliffs. Some said that having lived so long by the full beating of the sea, and where always the wind cries loudest, he could not feel the joys of other men, but only felt the sorrow of the sea crying in his soul for ever.

"Long ago on the path of stars, midmost between the worlds, there strode the gods of Old. In the bleak middle of the worlds They sat and the worlds went round and round, like dead leaves in the wind at Autumn's end, with never a life on one, while the gods went sighing for the things that might not be. And the centuries went over the gods to go where the centuries go, toward the End of Things, and with Them went the sighs of all the gods as They longed for what might not be.

"One by one in the midst of the worlds, fell dead the gods of Old, still sighing for the things that might not be, all slain by Their own regrets. Only Shimono Kani, the youngest of the gods, made him a harp out of the heart strings of all the elder gods, and, sitting upon the Path of Stars in the Middle of Things, played upon the harp a dirge for the gods of Old. And the song told of all vain regrets and of unhappy loves of the gods in the olden time, and of Their great deeds that were to adorn the future years. But into the dirge of Shimono Kani came voices crying out of the heart strings of the gods, all sighing still for the things that might not be. And the dirge and the voices crying, go drifting away from the Path of Stars, away from the Midst of Things, till they come twittering among the Worlds, like a great host of birds that are lost by night. And every note is a life, and many notes become caught up among the worlds to be entangled with flesh for a little while before they pass again on their journey to the great Anthem that roars at the End of Time.

Time and the Gods

Shimono Kani hath given a voice to the wind and added a sorrow to the sea. But when in lighted chambers after feasting there arises the voice of the singer to please the King, then is the soul of that singer crying aloud to his fellows from where he stands chained to earth. And when at the sound of the singing the heart of the King grows sad and his princes lament then they remember, though knowing not that, they remember it, the sad face of Shimono Kani sitting by his dead brethren, the elder gods, playing on the harp of crying heart strings whereby he sent their souls among the worlds.

"And when the music of one lute is lonely on the hills at night, then one soul calleth to his brother souls—the notes of Shimono Kani's dirge which have not been caught among the worlds—and he knoweth not to whom he calls or why, but knoweth only that minstrelsy is his only cry and sendeth it out into the dark.

"But although in the prison houses of earth all memories must die, yet as there sometimes clings to a prisoner's feet some dust of the fields wherein he was captured, so sometimes fragments of remembrance cling to a man's soul after it hath been taken to earth. Then a great minstrel arises, and, weaving together the shreds of his memories, maketh some melody such as the hand of Shimono Kani smites out of his harp; and they that pass by say: 'Hath there not been some such melody before?' and pass on sad at heart for memories which are not.

"Therefore, O King, one day the great gates of thy palace shall lie open for a procession wherein the King comes down to pass through a people, lamenting with lute and drum; and on the same day a prison door shall be opened by relenting hands, and one more lost note of Shimono Kani's dirge shall go back to swell his melody again.

"The dirge of Shimono Kani shall roll on till one day it shall come with all its notes complete to overwhelm the Silence that sits at the End of Things. Then shall Shimono Kani say to his brethren's bones: The things that might not be have at last become.'

"But very quiet shall be the bones of the gods of Old, and only Their voices shall live which cried from the harp of heart strings, for the things which might not be."

Time and the Gods

VI

When the caravans, saying farewell to Zandara, set out across the waste northwards towards Einandhu, they follow the desert track for seven days before they come to water where Shubah Onath rises black out of the waste, with a well at its foot and herbage on its summit. On this rock a prophet hath his Temple and is called the Prophet of Journeys, and hath carven in a southern window smiling along the camel track all gods that are benignant to caravans.

There a traveller may learn by prophecy whether he shall accomplish the ten days' journey thence across the desert and so come to the white city of Einandhu, or whether his bones shall lie with the bones of old along the desert track.

No name hath the Prophet of Journeys, for none is needed in that desert where no man calls nor ever a man answers.

Thus spake the Prophet of Journeys standing before the King:

"The journey of the King shall be an old journey pushed on apace.

"Many a year before the making of the moon thou camest down with dream camels from the City without a name that stands beyond all the stars. And then began thy journey over the Waste of Nought, and thy dream camel bore thee well when those of certain of thy fellow travellers fell down in the Waste and were covered over by the silence and were turned again to nought; and those travellers when their dream camels fell, having nothing to carry them further over the Waste, were lost beyond and never found the earth. These are those men that might have been but were not. And all about thee fluttered the myriad hours travelling in great swarms across the Waste of Nought.

"How many centuries passed across the cities while thou wast making thy journey none may reckon, for there is no time in the Waste of Nought, but only the hours fluttering earthwards from beyond to do the work of Time. At last the dream–borne travellers saw far off a green place gleaming and made haste towards it and so came to Earth. And there, O King, ye rest for a little while, thou and those that came with thee, making an encampment upon earth before journeying on. There the swarming hours alight, settling

83

on every blade of grass and tree, and spreading over your tents and devouring all things, and at last bending your very tent poles with their weight and wearying you.

"Behind the encampment in the shadow of the tents lurks a dark figure with a nimble sword, having the name of Time. This is he that hath called the hours from beyond and he it is that is their master, and it is his work that the hours do as they devour all green things upon the earth and tatter the tents and weary all the travellers. As each of the hours does the work of Time, Time smites him with his nimble sword as soon as his work is done, and the hour falls severed to the dust with his bright wings scattered, as a locust cut asunder by the scimitar of a skillful swordsman.

"One by one, O King, with a stir in the camp, and the folding up of the tents one by one, the travellers shall push on again on the journey begun so long before out of the City without a name to the place where dream camels go, striding free through the Waste. So into the Waste, O King, thou shalt set forth ere long, perhaps to renew friendships begun during thy short encampment upon earth.

"Other green places thou shalt meet in the Waste and thereon shalt encamp again until driven thence by the hours. What prophet shall relate how many journeys thou shalt make or how many encampments? But at last thou shalt come to the place of The Resting of Camels, and there shall gleaming cliffs that are named The Ending of Journeys lift up out of the Waste of Nought, Nought at their feet, Nought laying wide before them, with only the glint of worlds far off to illumine the Waste. One by one, on tired dream camels, the travellers shall come in, and going up the pathway through the cliff in that land of The Resting of Camels shall come on The City of Ceasing. There, the dream–wrought pinnacles and the spires that are builded of men's hopes shall rise up real before thee, seen only hitherto as a mirage in the Waste.

"So far the swarming hours may not come, and far away among the tents shall stand the dark figure with the nimble sword. But in the scintillant streets, under the song–built abodes of the last of cities, thy journey, O King, shall end."

VII

In the valley beyond Sidono there lies a garden of poppies, and where the poppies' heads are all a–swing with summer breezes that go up the valley there lies a path well strewn with ocean shells. Over Sidono's summit the birds come streaming to the lake that lies in the valley of the garden, and behind them rises the sun sending Sidono's shadow as far as the edge of the lake. And down the path of many ocean shells when they begin to gleam in the sun, every morning walks an aged man clad in a silken robe with strange devices woven. A little temple where the old man lives stands at the edge of the path. None worship there, for Zornadhu, the old prophet, hath forsaken men to walk among his poppies.

For Zornadhu hath failed to understand the purport of Kings and cities and the moving up and down of many people to the tune of the clinking of gold. Therefore hath Zornadhu gone far away from the sound of cities and from those that are ensnared thereby, and beyond Sidono's mountain hath come to rest where there are neither kings nor armies nor bartering for gold, but only the heads of the poppies that sway in the wind together and the birds that fly from Sidono to the lake, and then the sunrise over Sidono's summit; and afterwards the flight of birds out of the lake and over Sidono again, and sunset behind the valley, and high over lake and garden the stars that know not cities. There Zornadhu lives in his garden of poppies with Sidono standing between him and the whole world of men; and when the wind blowing athwart the valley sways the heads of the tall poppies against the Temple wall, the old prophet says: "The flowers are all praying, and lo! they be nearer to the gods than men."

But the heralds of the King coming after many days of travel to Sidono perceived the garden valley. By the lake they saw the poppy garden gleaming round and small like a sunrise over water on a misty morning seen by some shepherd from the hills. And descending the bare mountain for three days they came to the gaunt pines, and ever between the tall trunks came the glare of the poppies that shone from the garden valley. For a whole day they travelled through the pines. That night a cold wind came up the garden valley crying against the poppies. Low in his Temple, with a song of exceeding grief, Zornadhu in the morning made a dirge for the passing of poppies, because in the night time there had fallen petals that might not return or ever come again into the garden valley. Outside the Temple on the path of ocean shells the heralds halted, and read the names and honours of the King; and from the Temple came the voice of Zornadhu still singing his lament. But they took him from his garden because of the King's command, and down his gleaming path of ocean shells and away up Sidono, and left the Temple empty with none to lament when silken poppies died. And the will of the wind of the

85

autumn was wrought upon the poppies, and the heads of the poppies that rose from the earth went down to the earth again, as the plume of a warrior smitten in a heathen fight far away, where there are none to lament him. Thus out of his land of flowers went Zornadhu and came perforce into the lands of men, and saw cities, and in the city's midst stood up before the King.

And the King said:

"Zornadhu, what of the journey of the King and of the princes and the people that shall meet me?"

Zornadhu answered:

"I know nought of Kings, but in the night time the poppy made his journey a little before dawn. Thereafter the wildfowl came as is their wont over Sidono's summit, and the sun rising behind them gleamed upon Sidono, and all the flowers of the lake awoke. And the bee passing up and down the garden went droning to other poppies, and the flowers of the lake, they that had known the poppy, knew him no more. And the sun's rays slanting from Sidono's crest lit still a garden valley where one poppy waved his petals to the dawn no more. And I, O King, that down a path of gleaming ocean shells walk in the morning, found not, nor have since found, that poppy again, that hath gone on the journey whence there is not returning, out of my garden valley. And I, O King, made a dirge to cry beyond that valley and the poppies bowed their heads; but there is no cry nor no lament that may adjure the life to return again to a flower that grew in a garden once and hereafter is not.

"Unto what place the lives of poppies have gone no man shall truly say. Sure it is that to that place are only outward tracks. Only it may be that when a man dreams at evening in a garden where heavily the scent of poppies hangs in the air, when the winds have sunk, and far away the sound of a lute is heard on lonely hills, as he dreams of silken-scarlet poppies that once were a-swing together in the gardens of his youth, the lives of those old lost poppies shall return, living again in his dream. *So there may dream the gods.* And through the dreams of some divinity reclining in tinted fields above the morning we may haply pass again, although our bodies have long swirled up and down the world with other dust. In these strange dreams our lives may be again, all in the centre of our hopes, rejoicings and laments, until above the morning the gods wake to go about their work, haply to remember still Their idle dreams, haply to dream them all again in the stillness when shines the starlight of the gods."

VIII

Then said the King: "I like not these strange journeys nor this faint wandering through the dreams of gods like the shadow of a weary camel that may not rest when the sun is low. The gods that have made me to love the earth's cool woods and dancing streams do ill to send me into the starry spaces that I love not, with my soul still peering earthward through the eternal years, as a beggar who once was noble staring from the street at lighted halls. For wherever the gods may send me I shall be as the gods have made me, a creature loving the green fields of earth.

"Now if there stand one prophet here that hath the ear of those too splendid gods that stride above the glories of the orient sky, tell them that there is on earth one King in the land called Zarkandhu to the south of the opal mountains, who would fain tarry among the many gardens of earth, and would leave to other men the splendours that the gods shall give the dead above the twilight that surrounds the stars."

Then spake Yamen, prophet of the Temple of Obin that stands on the shores of a great lake, facing east. Yamen said: "I pray oft to the gods who sit above the twilight behind the east. When the clouds are heavy and red at sunset, or when there is boding of thunder or eclipse, then I pray not, lest my prayers be scattered and beaten earthward. But when the sun sets in a tranquil sky, pale green or azure, and the light of his farewells stays long upon lonely hills, then I send forth my prayers to flutter upward to gods that are surely smiling, and the gods hear my prayers. But, O King, boons sought out of due time from the gods are never wholly to be desired, and, if They should grant to thee to tarry on the earth, old age would trouble thee with burdens more and more till thou wouldst become the driven slave of the hours in fetters that none may break."

The King said: "They that have devised this burden of age may surely stay it, pray therefore on the calmest evening of the year to the gods above the twilight that I may tarry always on the earth and always young, while over my head the scourges of the gods pass and alight not."

87

Time and the Gods

Then answered Yamen: "The King hath commanded, yet among the blessings of the gods there always cries a curse. The great princes that make merry with the King, who tell of the great deeds that the King wrought in the former time, shall one by one grow old. And thou, O King, seated at the feast crying, 'make merry' and extolling the former time shall find about thee white heads nodding in sleep, and men that are forgetting the former time. Then one by one the names of those that sported with thee once called by the gods, one by one the names of the singers that sing the songs thou lovest called by the gods, lastly of those that chased the grey boar by night and took him in Orghoom river—only the King. Then a new people that have not known the old deeds of the King nor fought and chased with him, who dare not make merry with the King as did his long dead princes. And all the while those princes that are dead growing dearer and greater in thy memory, and all the while the men that served thee then growing more small to thee. And all the old things fading and new things arising which are not as the old things were, the world changing yearly before thine eyes and the gardens of thy childhood overgrown. Because thy childhood was in the olden years thou shalt love the olden years, but ever the new years shall overthrow them and their customs, and not the will of a King may stay the changes that the gods have planned for all the customs of old. Ever thou shalt say 'This was not so,' and ever the new custom shall prevail even against a King. When thou hast made merry a thousand times thou shalt grow tired of making merry. At last thou shalt become weary of the chase, and still old age shall not come near to thee to stifle desires that have been too oft fulfilled; then, O King, thou shalt be a hunter yearning for the chase but with nought to pursue that hath not been oft overcome. Old age shall come not to bury thine ambitions in a time when there is nought for thee to aspire to any more. Experience of many centuries shall make thee wise but hard and very sad, and thou shalt be a mind apart from thy fellows and curse them all for fools, and they shall not perceive thy wisdom because thy thoughts are not their thoughts and the gods that they have made are not the gods of the olden time. No solace shall thy wisdom bring thee but only an increasing knowledge that thou knowest nought, and thou shalt feel as a wise man in a world of fools, or else as a fool in a world of wise men, when all men feel so sure and ever thy doubts increase. When all that spake with thee of thine old deeds are dead, those that saw them not shall speak of them again to thee; till one speaking to thee of thy deeds of valour add more than even a man should when speaking to a King, and thou shalt suddenly doubt whether these great deeds were; and there shall be none to tell thee, only the echoes of the voices of the gods still singing in thine ears when long ago They called the princes that were thy friends. And thou shalt hear the knowledge of the olden time most wrongly told and afterwards forgotten. Then many prophets shall arise claiming discovery of that old knowledge. Then thou shalt find that seeking knowledge is vain, as the chase is vain, as making merry is vain, as all things are vain. One day thou shalt find that it is vain to be a King. Greatly then will the acclamations of the people weary thee, till the time when people grow aweary of Kings. Then thou shalt know that thou hast been uprooted from thine olden time and set to live in uncongenial years, and jests all new to royal ears shall smite thee on the head like hailstones, when thou hast lost thy crown, when those to whose grandsires thou hadst granted to bring them as children to kiss the feet of the King shall mock at thee because thou hast not learnt to barter with gold.

"Not all the marvels of the future time shall atone to thee for those old memories that glow warmer and brighter every year as they recede into the ages that the gods have gathered. And always dreaming of thy long dead princes and of the great Kings of other kingdoms in the olden time thou shalt fail to see the grandeur to which a hurrying jesting people shall attain in that kingless age. Lastly, O King, thou shalt perceive men changing in a way that thou shalt not comprehend, knowing what thou canst not know, till thou shalt discover that these are men no more and a new race holds dominion over the earth whose forefathers were men. These shall speak to thee no more as they hurry upon a quest that thou shalt never understand, and thou shalt know that thou canst no longer take thy part in shaping destinies, but in a world of cities only pine for air and the waving grass again and the sound of a wind in trees. Then even this shall end with the shapes of the gods in the darkness gathering all lives but thine, when the hills shall fling up earth's long stored heat back to the heavens again, when earth shall be old and cold, with nothing alive upon it but one King."

Then said the King: "Pray to those hard gods still, for those that have loved the earth with all its gardens and woods and singing streams will love earth still when it is old and cold and with all its gardens gone and all the purport of its being failed and nought but memories."

IX

Then spake Paharn, a prophet of the land of Hurn.

And Paharn said:

Time and the Gods

"There was one man that knew, but he stands not here."

And the King said:

"Is he further than my heralds might travel in the night if they went upon fleet horses?"

And the prophet answered:

"He is no further than thy heralds may well travel in the night, but further than they may return from in all the years. Out of this city there goes a valley wandering through all the world and opens out at last on the green land of Hurn. On the one side in the distance gleams the sea, and on the other side a forest, black and ancient, darkens the fields of Hurn; beyond the forest and the sea there is no more, saving the twilight and beyond that the gods. In the mouth of the valley sleeps the village of Rhistaun.

"Here I was born, and heard the murmur of the flocks and herds, and saw the tall smoke standing between the sky and the still roofs of Rhistaun, and learned that men might not go into the dark forest, and that beyond the forest and the sea was nought saving the twilight, and beyond that the gods. Often there came travellers from the world all down the winding valley, and spake with strange speech in Rhistaun and returned again up the valley going back to the world. Sometimes with bells and camels and men running on foot, Kings came down the valley from the world, but always the travellers returned by the valley again and none went further than the land of Hurn.

"And Kithneb also was born in the land of Hurn and tended the flocks with me, but Kithneb would not care to listen to the murmur of the flocks and herds and see the tall smoke standing between the roofs and the sky, but needed to know how far from Hurn it was that the world met the twilight, and how far across the twilight sat the gods.

"And often Kithneb dreamed as he tended the flocks and herds, and when others slept he would wander near to the edge of the forest wherein men might not go. And the elders of the land of Hurn reproved Kithneb when he dreamed; yet Kithneb was still as other men and mingled with his fellows until the day of which I will tell thee, O King. For Kithneb was aged about a score of years, and he and I were sitting near the flocks, and he gazed long at the point where the dark forest met the sea at the end of the land of Hurn. But when night drove the twilight down under the forest we brought the flocks together to

90

Time and the Gods

Rhistaun, and I went up the street between the houses to see four princes that had come down the valley from the world, and they were clad in blue and scarlet and wore plumes upon their heads, and they gave us in exchange for our sheep some gleaming stones which they told us were of great value on the word of princes. And I sold them three sheep, and Darniag sold them eight.

"But Kithneb came not with the others to the market place where the four princes stood, but went alone across the fields to the edge of the forest.

"And it was upon the next morning that the strange thing befell Kithneb; for I saw him in the morning coming from the fields, and I hailed him with the shepherd's cry wherewith we shepherds call to one another, and he answered not. Then I stopped and spake to him, and Kithneb said not a word till I became angry and left him.

"Then we spake together concerning Kithneb, and others had hailed him, and he had not answered them, but to one he had said that he had heard the voices of the gods speaking beyond the forest and so would never listen more to the voices of men.

"Then we said: 'Kithneb is mad,' and none hindered him.

"Another took his place among the flocks, and Kithneb sat in the evenings by the edge of the forest on the plain, alone.

"So Kithneb spake to none for many days, but when any forced him to speak he said that every evening he heard the gods when they came to sit in the forest from over the twilight and sea, and that he would speak no more with men.

"But as the months went by, men in Rhistaun came to look on Kithneb as a prophet, and we were wont to point to him when strangers came down the valley from the world, saying:

"'Here in the land of Hurn we have a prophet such as you have not among your cities, for he speaks at evening with the gods.'

"A year had passed over the silence of Kithneb when he came to me and spake. And I bowed before him because we believed that he spake among the gods. And Kithneb said:

Time and the Gods

"'I will speak to thee before the end because I am most lonely. For how may I speak again with men and women in the little streets of Rhistaun among the houses, when I have heard the voices of the gods singing above the twilight? But I am more lonely than ever Rhistaun wonts of, for this I tell thee, *when I hear the gods I know not what They say.* Well indeed I know the voice of each, for ever calling me away from contentment; well I know Their voices as they call to my soul and trouble it; I know by Their tone when They rejoice, and I know when They are sad, for even the gods feel sadness. I know when over fallen cities of the past, and the curved white bones of heroes They sing the dirges of the gods' lament. But alas! Their words I know not, and the wonderful strains of the melody of Their speech beat on my soul and pass away unknown.

"'Therefore I travelled from the land of Hurn till I came to the house of the prophet Arnin−Yo, and told him that I sought to find the meaning of the gods; and Arnin−Yo told me to ask the shepherds concerning all the gods, for what the shepherds knew it was meet for a man to know, and, beyond that, knowledge turned into trouble.

"'But I told Arnin−Yo that I had heard myself the voices of the gods and knew that They were there beyond the twilight and so could never more bow down to the gods that the shepherds made from the red clay which they scooped with their hands out of the hillside.

"'Then said Arnin−Yo to me:

"'"Natheless forget that thou hast heard the gods and bow down again to the gods of the red clay that the shepherds make, and find thereby the ease that the shepherds find, and at last die, remembering devoutly the gods of the red clay that the shepherds scooped with their hands out of the hill. For the gifts of the gods that sit beyond the twilight and smile at the gods of clay, are neither ease nor contentment."

"'And I said:

"'"The god that my mother made out of the red clay that she had got from the hill, fashioning it with many arms and eyes as she sang me songs of its power, and told me stories of its mystic birth, this god is lost and broken; and ever in my ears is ringing the melody of the gods."

"'And Arnin−Yo said:

92

Time and the Gods

""If thou wouldst still seek knowledge know that only those that come behind the gods may clearly know their meaning. And this thou canst only do by taking ship and putting out to sea from the land of Hurn and sailing up the coast towards the forest. There the sea cliffs turn to the left or southward, and full upon them beats the twilight from over the sea, and there thou mayest come round behind the forest. Here where the world's edge mingles with the twilight the gods come in the evening, and if thou canst come behind Them thou shalt hear Their voices clear, beating full seaward and filling all the twilight with sound of song, and thou shalt know the meaning of the gods. But where the cliffs turn southward there sits behind the gods Brimdono, the oldest whirlpool in the sea, roaring to guard his masters. Him the gods have chained for ever to the floor of the twilit sea to guard the door of the forest that lieth above the cliffs. Here, then, if thou canst hear the voices of the gods as thou hast said, thou wilt know their meaning clear, but this will profit thee little when Brimdono drags thee down and all thy ship.'"

"Thus spake Kithneb to me.

"But I said:

"'O Kithneb, forget those whirlpool–guarded gods beyond the forest, and if thy small god be lost thou shalt worship with me the small god that my mother made. Thousands of years ago he conquered cities but is not any longer an angry god. Pray to him, Kithneb, and he shall bring thee comfort and increase to thy flocks and a mild spring, and at the last a quiet ending for thy days.'

"But Kithneb heeded not, and only bade me find a fisher ship and men to row it. So on the next day we put forth from the land of Hurn in a boat that the fisher folk use. And with us came four of the fisher folk who rowed the boat while I held the rudder, but Kithneb sat and spake not in the prow. And we rowed westward up the coast till we came at evening where the cliffs turned southward and the twilight gleamed upon them and the sea.

"There we turned southwards and saw at once Brimdono. And as a man tears the purple cloak of a king slain in battle to divide it with other warriors,—Brimdono tore the sea. And ever around and around him with a gnarled hand Brimdono whirled the sail of some adventurous ship, the trophy of some calamity wrought in his greed for shipwreck long ago where he sat to guard his masters from all who fare on the sea. And ever one far—reaching empty hand swung up and down so that we durst go no nearer.

"Only Kithneb neither saw Brimdono nor heard his roar, and when we would go no further bade us lower a small boat with oars out of the ship. Into this boat Kithneb descended, not heeding words from us, and onward rowed alone. A cry of triumph over ships and men Brimdono uttered before him, but Kithneb's eyes were turned toward the forest as he came behind the gods. Upon his face the twilight beat full from the haunts of evening to illumine the smiles that grew about his eyes as he came behind the gods. Him that had found the gods above Their twilit cliffs, him that had heard Their voices close at last and knew Their meaning clear, him, from the cheerless world with its doubtings and prophets that lie, from all hidden meanings, where truth rang clear at last, Brimdono took."

But when Paharn ceased to speak, in the King's ears the roar of Brimdono exulting over ancient triumphs and the whelming of ships seemed still to ring.

X

Then Mohontis spake, the hermit prophet, who lived in the deep untravelled woods that seclude Lake Ilana.

"I dreamed that to the west of all the seas I saw by vision the mouth of Munra—O, guarded by golden gates, and through the bars of the gates that guard the mysterious river of Munra—O I saw the flashes of golden barques, wherein the gods went up and down, and to and fro through the evening dusk. And I saw that Munra—O was a river of dreams such as came through remembered gardens in the night, to charm our infancy as we slept beneath the sloping gables of the houses of long ago. And Munra—O rolled down her dreams from the unknown inner land and slid them under the golden gates and out into the waste, unheeding sea, till they beat far off upon low—lying shores and murmured songs of long ago to the islands of the south, or shouted tumultuous paeans to the Northern crags; or cried forlornly against rocks where no one came, dreams that might not be dreamed.

"Many gods there be, that through the dusk of an evening in the summer go up and down this river. There I saw, in a high barque all of gold, gods the of the pomp of cities; there I

94

Time and the Gods

saw gods of splendour, in boats bejewelled to the keels; gods of magnificence and gods of power. I saw the dark ships and the glint of steel of the gods whose trade was war, and I heard the melody of the bells of silver arow in the rigging of harpstrings as the gods of melody went sailing through the dusk on the river of Munra—O. Wonderful river of Munra—O! I saw a grey ship with sails of the spider's web all lit with dewdrop lanterns, and on its prow was a scarlet cock with its wings spread far and wide when the gods of the dawn sailed also on Munra–O.

"Down this river it is the wont of the gods to carry the souls of men eastward to where the world in the distance faces on Munra–O. Then I knew that when the gods of the Pride of Power and gods of the Pomp of Cities went down the river in their tall gold ships to take earthward other souls, swiftly adown the river and between the ships had gone in this boat of birch bark the god Tarn, the hunter, bearing my soul to the world. And I know now that he came down the stream in the dusk keeping well to the middle, and that he moved silently and swiftly among the ships, wielding a twin–bladed oar. I remember, now, the yellow gleaming of the great boats of the gods of the Pomp of Cities, and the huge prow above me of the gods of the Pride of Power, when Tarn, dipping his right blade into the river, lifted his left blade high, and the drops gleamed and fell. Thus Tarn the hunter took me to the world that faces across the sea of the west on the gate of Munra–O. And so it was that there grew upon me the glamour of the hunt, though I had forgotten Tarn, and took me into mossy places and into dark woods, and I became the cousin of the wolf and looked into the lynx's eyes and knew the bear; and the birds called to me with half–remembered notes, and there grew in me a deep love of great rivers and of all western seas, and a distrust of cities, and all the while I had forgotten Tarn.

"I know not what high galleon shall come for thee, O King, nor what rowers, clad with purple, shall row at the bidding of gods when thou goest back with pomp to the river of Munra–O. But for me Tarn waits where the Seas of the West break over the edge of the world, and, as the years pass over me and the love of the chase sinks low, and as the glamour of the dark woods and mossy places dies down in my soul, ever louder and louder lap the ripples against the canoe of birch bark where, holding his twin–bladed oar, Tarn waits.

"But when my soul hath no more knowledge of the woods nor kindred any longer with the creatures of the dark, and when all that Tarn hath given it shall be lost, then Tarn shall take me back over the western seas, where all the remembered years lie floating idly aswing with the ebb and flow, to bring me again to the river of Munra–O. Far up that river we shall haply chase those creatures whose eyes are peering in the night as they prowl around the world, for Tarn was ever a hunter."

XI

Then Ulf spake, the prophet who in Sistrameides lives in a temple anciently dedicated to the gods. Rumour hath guessed that there the gods walked once some time towards evening. But Time whose hand is against the temples of the gods hath dealt harshly with it and overturned its pillars and set upon its ruins his sign and seal: now Ulf dwells there alone. And Ulf said, "There sets, O King, a river outward from earth which meets with a mighty sea whose waters roll through space and fling their billows on the shores of every star. These are the river and the sea of the Tears of Men."

And the King said:

"Men have not written of this sea."

And the prophet answered:

"Have not tears enough burst in the night time out of sleeping cities? Have not the sorrows of 10,000 homes sent streams into this river when twilight fell and it was still and there was none to hear? Have there not been hopes, and were they all fulfilled? Have there not been conquests and bitter defeats? And have not flowers when spring was over died in the gardens of many children? Tears enough, O King, tears enough have gone down out of earth to make such a sea; and deep it is and wide and the gods know it and it flings its spray on the shores of all the stars. Down this river and across this sea thou shalt fare in a ship of sighs and all around thee over the sea shall fly the prayers of men which rise on white wings higher than their sorrows. Sometimes perched in the rigging, sometimes crying around thee, shall go the prayers that availed not to stay thee in Zarkandhu. Far over the waters, and on the wings of the prayers beats the light of an inaccessible star. No hand hath touched it, none hath journeyed to it, it hath no substance, it is only a light, it is the star of Hope, and it shines far over the sea and brightens the world. It is nought but a light, but the gods gave it.

Time and the Gods

"Led only by the light of this star the myriad prayers that thou shalt see all around thee fly to the Hall of the gods.

"Sighs shall waft thy ship of sighs over the sea of Tears. Thou shalt pass by islands of laughter and lands of song lying low in the sea, and all of them drenched with tears flung over their rocks by the waves of the sea all driven by the sighs.

"But at last thou shalt come with the prayers of men to the great Hall of the gods where the chairs of the gods are carved of onyx grouped round the golden throne of the eldest of the gods. And there, O King, hope not to find the gods, but reclining upon the golden throne wearing a cloak of his master's thou shalt see the figure of Time with blood upon his hands, and loosely dangling from his fingers a dripping sword, and spattered with blood but empty shall stand the onyx chairs.

"There he sits on his master's throne dangling idly his sword, or with it flicking cruelly at the prayers of men that lie in a great heap bleeding at his feet.

"For a while, O King, the gods had sought to solve the riddles of Time, for a while They made him Their slave, and Time smiled and obeyed his masters, for a while, O King, for a while. He that hath spared nothing hath not spared the gods, nor yet shall he spare thee."

Then the King spake dolefully in the Hall of Kings, and said:

"May I not find at last the gods, and must it be that I may not look in Their faces at the last to see whether They be kindly? They that have sent me on my earthward journey I would greet on my returning, if not as a King coming again to his own city, yet as one who having been ordered had obeyed, and obeying had merited something of those for whom he toiled. I would look Them in Their faces, O prophet, and ask Them concerning many things and would know the wherefore of much. I had hoped, O prophet, that those gods that had smiled upon my childhood, Whose voices stirred at evening in gardens when I was young, would hold dominion still when at last I came to seek Them. O prophet, if this is not to be, make you a great dirge for my childhood's gods and fashion silver bells and, setting them mostly a–swing amidst such trees as grew in the garden of my childhood, sing you this dirge in the dusk: and sing it when the low moth flies up and down and the bat first comes peering from her home, sing it when white mists come rising from the river, when smoke is pale and grey, while flowers are yet closing, ere voices are yet hushed, sing it while all things yet lament the day, or ever the great lights of heaven come blazing forth and night with her splendours takes the place of day. For, if the old gods die, let us lament Them or ever new knowledge comes, while all the world still shudders at Their loss.

"For at the last, O prophet, what is left? Only the gods of my childhood dead, and only Time striding large and lonely through the spaces, chilling the moon and paling the light of stars and scattering earthward out of both his hands the dust of forgetfulness over the fields of heroes and smitten Temples of the older gods."

But when the other prophets heard with what doleful words the King spake in the Hall they all cried out:

"It is not as Ulf has said but as I have said—and I."

Then the King pondered long, not speaking. But down in the city in a street between the houses stood grouped together they that were wont to dance before the King, and they that had borne his wine in jewelled cups. Long they had tarried in the city hoping that the King might relent, and once again regard them with kindly faces calling for wine and song. The next morning they were all to set out in search of some new Kingdom, and they were peering between the houses and up the long grey street to see for the last time the palace of King Ebalon; and Pattering Leaves, the dancer, cried:

"Not any more, not any more at all shall we drift up the carven hall to dance before the King. He that now watches the magic of his prophets will behold no more the wonder of the dance, and among ancient parchments, strange and wise, he shall forget the swirl of drapery when we swing together through the Dance of the Myriad Steps."

And with her were Silvern Fountain and Summer Lightning and Dream of the Sea, each lamenting that they should dance no more to please the eyes of the King.

And Intahn who had carried at the banquet for fifty years the goblet of the King set with its four sapphires each as large as an eye, said as he spread his hands towards the palace making the sign of farewell:

"Not all the magic of prophecy nor yet foreseeing nor perceiving may equal the power of wine. Through the small door in the King's Hall one goes by one hundred steps and many sloping corridors into the cool of the earth where lies a cavern vaster than the Hall. Therein, curtained by the spider, repose the casks of wine that are wont to gladden the hearts of the Kings of Zarkandhu. In islands far to the eastward the vine, from whose heart this wine was long since wrung, hath climbed aloft with many a clutching finger and beheld the sea and ships of the olden time and men since dead, and gone down into the earth again and been covered over with weeds. And green with the damp of years there lie three casks that a city gave not up until all her defenders were slain and her houses fired; and ever to the soul of that wine is added a more ardent fire as ever the years go by. Thither it was my pride to go before a banquet in the olden years, and coming up to bear in the sapphire goblet the fire of the elder Kings and to watch the King's eye flash and his face grow nobler and more like his sires as he drank the gleaming wine.

"And now the King seeks wisdom from his prophets while all the glory of the past and all the clattering splendour of today grows old, far down, forgotten beneath his feet."

And when he ceased the cupbearers and the women that danced looked long in silence at the palace. Then one by one all made the farewell sign before they turned to go, and as they did this a herald unseen in the dark was speeding towards them.

After a long silence the King spake:

"Prophets of my Kingdom," he said, "you have not prophesied alike, and the words of each prophet condemn his fellows' words so that wisdom may not be discovered among prophets. But I command that none in my Kingdom shall doubt that the earliest King of Zarkandhu stored wine beneath this palace before the building of the city or ever the palace arose, and I shall cause commands to be uttered for the making of a banquet at once within this Hall, so that ye shall perceive that the power of my wine is greater than all your spells, and dancing more wondrous than prophecy."

The dancers and the winebearers were summoned back, and as the night wore on a banquet was spread and all the prophets bidden to be seated, Samahn, Ynath, Monith, Ynar Thun, the prophet of Journeys, Zornadhu, Yamen, Paharn, Ilana, Ulf, and one that had not spoken nor yet revealed his name, and who wore his prophet's cloak across his face.

And the prophets feasted as they were commanded and spake as other men spake, save he whose face was hidden, who neither ate nor spake. Once he put out his hand from under his cloak and touched a blossom among the flowers upon the table and the blossom fell.

And Pattering Leaves came in and danced again, and the King smiled, and Pattering Leaves was happy though she had not the wisdom of the prophets. And in and out, in and out, in and out among the columns of the Hall went Summer Lightning in the maze of the dance. And Silvern Fountain bowed before the King and danced and danced and bowed again, and old Intahn went to and fro from the cavern to the King gravely through the midst of the dancers but with kindly eyes, and when the King had often drunk of the old wine of the elder Kings he called for Dream of the Sea and bade her sing. And Dream of the Sea came through the arches and sang of an island builded by magic out of pearls, that lay set in a ruby sea, and how it lay far off and under the south, guarded by jagged reefs whereon the sorrows of the world were wrecked and never came to the island. And how a low sunset always reddened the sea and lit the magic isle and never turned to night, and how someone sang always and endlessly to lure the soul of a King who might by enchantment pass the guarding reefs to find rest on the pearl island and not be troubled more, but only see sorrows on the outer reef battered and broken. Then Soul of the South rose up and sang a song of a fountain that ever sought to reach the sky and was ever doomed to fall to the earth again until at last....

Then whether it was the art of Pattering Leaves or the song of Dream of the Sea, or whether it was the fire of the wine of the elder Kings, Ebalon bade farewell kindly to the prophets when morning paled the stars. Then along the torchlit corridors the King went to his chamber, and having shut the door in the empty room, beheld suddenly a figure wearing the cloak of a prophet; and the King perceived that it was he whose face was hidden at the banquet, who had not revealed his name.

And the King said:

"Art thou, too, a prophet?"

And the figure answered:

100

"I am a prophet."

And the King said: "Knowest *thou* aught concerning the journey of the King?" And the figure answered: "I know, but have never said."

And the King said: "Who art thou that knowest so much and has not told it?"

And he answered:

"I am *The End*."

Then the cloaked figure strode away from the palace; and the King, unseen by the guards, followed upon his journey.

THE END

Printed in the United States
53652LVS00004B/87-156